P9-DKF-912

how to be brave

how to be brave

E. KATHERINE KOTTARAS

to be

brave

ST. MARTIN'S GRIFFIN
NEW YORK

This is a work of fiction. All of the characters, organizations, and events portrayed in this novel are either products of the author's imagination or are used fictitiously.

HOW TO BE BRAVE. Copyright © 2015 by E. Katherine Kottaras. All rights reserved. Printed in the United States of America. For information, address St. Martin's Press, 175 Fifth Avenue, New York, N.Y. 10010.

www.stmartins.com

Grateful acknowledgment is made to the authors to reproduce from the following:

Carol S. Eliel, Lee Mullican, Amy Gerstler, and Lari Pittman,
Lee Mullican: An Abundant Harvest of Sun (Los Angeles:
Los Angeles County Museum of Art, 2005).

The Library of Congress Cataloging-in-Publication Data is available upon request.

ISBN 978-1-250-07280-1 (hardcover)
ISBN 978-1-4668-8467-0 (e-book)

Our books may be purchased in bulk for promotional, educational, or business use. Please contact your local bookseller or the Macmillan Corporate and Premium Sales Department at (800) 221-7945, extension 5442, or by e-mail at MacmillanSpecialMarkets@macmillan .com.

First Edition: November 2015

10 9 8 7 6 5 4 3 2 1

For Madeline and Matthew

I've been absolutely terrified every moment of my life and I've never let it keep me from doing a single thing that I wanted to do.

—Georgia O'Keeffe

part one

1

This is what it was like:

> I didn't want you to come. I didn't want you there.
> The day before school, the very first year,
> we waited in line for my schedule.

> They stared. Those in line around us—
> the other girls and their moms,
> the ones who were my year,
> who were never my friends—
> They saw how you were big, planetary, next to them.
> Next to me.

> The girl in pigtails, someone's sister,
> asked: *Is there a baby inside?*
> Her mother, red now, whispered in her ear.

But the girl didn't mind:
Oh, so she's fat.

The other girls, the ones who were my year
who were never my friends—they laughed at you,
    quietly.
At me.

Her mother said she was sorry, so sorry,
And you said: *It's fine. It's fine.*
But it wasn't.

You squeezed my hand, and then to the girl in pigtails,
    you said: *I am big, yes. But I am beautiful, too.*
And so are you.

Her mother pulled her child away.
She left the line and let us go first.

I didn't say: *You shouldn't have come.*
I didn't say: *I don't want you here.*

But I also didn't say: *I love you.*
Or: *Thank you for being brave.*

Later that night, I cried:
I don't want to go. I don't want to face them.
And every year after.

You'd look at me like I was that girl,
and you'd say, as though it were true:
You are possibility and change and beauty.
One day, you will have a life, a beautiful life.
You will shine.

I didn't see it. I couldn't see it,
not in myself,
not in you.

Now, it's not like that anymore.

This is what it's like:

It's quiet in our house. Too quiet. Especially tonight.
The day before my first day of senior year.

The A/C hums, the fridge hums, the traffic hums.

I'm standing at my closet door, those old knots churning inside my stomach again.

I don't want to go tomorrow.

I need to talk to her.

Instead, I've done what she always did for me the night before the first day of the school year. I've picked out three complete outfits, hung them on my closet door.

It's a good start, I guess.

Outfit #1: Dark indigo skinny jeans (are they still considered skinny if they're a size 16?), drapey black shirt, long gold chain necklace that Liss gave me, and cheap ballet flats that hurt my feet because they're way too flat and I hate wearing shoes with no socks.

Outfit #2: Black leggings, dark blue drapey knee-length dress (draping is my thing), gold hoop earrings that belonged to my mom, and open-toed black sandals, but that would mean a last-minute half-assed pedicure tonight. A spedicure, if you will.

Outfit #3: A dress my mom bought for me two years ago. The Orange Dress. Well, really more like coral. With embroidered ribbons etched in angular lines that camouflage my flab. Knee-length (not too short/not too long). Three-quarter-length sleeves (to hide the sagging). It's perfectly retro. And just so beautiful. Especially with this utterly uncomfortable pair of canary-colored peep-toe pumps that belonged to my mom.

I begged her for the dress. I made her pay the $125 for it.

I knew my parents didn't have the money, but I couldn't help crying when I saw myself in the mirror. It fit (it's a size 14), and I think she saw how pretty I felt because I did feel pretty for the first time, so she charged it.

But I've never worn it.

The day after, she went into the ER, her heart acting up again. She needed another emergency stent, which meant more dye through her kidneys, which meant dialysis a few weeks later, which meant the beginning of the end of everything.

I never put it on after that.

It's just so bright. So unlike everything else I wear.

I could wear it tomorrow.

I could. And if she were here, she would tell me to.

I really need to talk to her.

It's just so quiet in this house.

My dad's in the living room, in his spot on the farthest end of the old couch, fists clenched tight, watching the muted TV. If he's not at the restaurant, he's there, sitting in the dark, staring at silent, flashing images. Watching the Cubs lose again or counting murders on the news or falling asleep to old John Wayne movies on AMC (no commercials). I sit down next to him.

The worn leather is cold against my calves.

I hear my mother's voice: *John Askeridis came to this country in 1972. He had to borrow money only once. He worked his way up from nothing. A self-made man. He was suave. Refined. A true Greek gentleman.*

Now he looks old and worn and lost.

"Give me your hand, Dad."

He looks at me, his eyebrows furrowed.

"Unclench your hands." I pull apart his clenched hand, force him to relax. "You know it's not good for you." *You know it's what she would have done.*

He lifts his hand and pulls at my nose. "Don't worry, *koúkla*. You worry too much about me." He takes me by the wrist, and I sink down into the couch next to him. He wraps his arm around my neck. I'm ten years old again. I'm safe here, with him. We're okay without her. *It's all going to be okay.*

"Dad, come on. Get up from the couch. Let's go do

something. Let's get out of here, go get dinner or something." *Let's be brave.*

"*Georgiamou*, you go. Go with your friends." He sighs
and turns his gaze back to the TV. "I've nothing to do."

Monday morning, 6:45 A.M. Clybourn and Fullerton,
waiting for the 74 bus. It's been ten minutes. The sun is
already burning hot on my skin. Stupid CTA. Chicago
public transit wants to ruin my life.

I check my phone for a bus update. I can't be late on
my first day. They'll give me detention. They got so strict
at the end of last year. But they wouldn't do it on the first
day, would they?

Shit. There I go again. Always expecting the worst.

Her letter is in my bag. I rub the folds of paper between
my fingers, close my eyes to imagine my mom's pen
running over it, her wrist touching the paper.

I'm trying to think positively. To be brave.

Okay, here goes. Positive Thought #1: I did it. I'm
wearing the Orange Dress.

I didn't sleep much last night. I stayed up reading and
I dozed off maybe around three A.M. When the alarm
went off at six, I opened my eyes, and it called out to me.
I jumped out from under the sheets and ripped off the
price tag.

Today's the day to start all over. Today's the day to start
living for her.

My bus arrives. I slide my card through the slot, and
the crusty old driver tips his hat to me. "Look at that

smile! The sun just got himself a reason to shine, little lady."

Well, there's Positive Thought #2. Thanks, crusty old man. I needed that.

I get off the bus to the sound of the first warning bell blaring two blocks away. I'm sure the swarming masses of eager freshies (and somewhat less so sophomores and juniors) are already filed like cattle at the front gate, shuffling through the metal detector. Principal Q-tip is probably standing at the gate, champing at the bit to sign us up for detention. Especially for us seniors. I'm nearly knocked over by a couple of guys who are racing down the sidewalk. I refuse to run. Not today. Not in these shoes.

I try my best to stride gracefully across the concrete, to Own This Dress, never mind the beads of sweat pouring down my back.

"Hey, *Ass*-keridis."

Avery Trenholm and her posse with their Hollister/ A&F/PINK ad-shirts, who've never had to work for anything, not a pair of jeans, not a grade (when your mom's a doctor and your dad's an engineer, shit like trigonometry and physics is encoded into your DNA), and certainly not their matching diamond-encrusted lockets.

Avery flips her sleek, straight hair. "Nice dress." Except she doesn't mean it. She'd never be caught dead in a dress like this. She's wearing these hideous nearly microscopic fringed denim shorts that might fit around my one ankle.

"Yeah." Chloe, Avery's slender and air-brained bitchy-junior-wannabe sidekick, gives me a once-over and says, "It's so, um, vivid." I don't know why she has anything to say. We've never exchanged more than two words to each other.

I keep moving forward. The second warning bell rings. Left foot, right foot. Left foot, right foot. Positive thoughts. Positive thoughts. Get to the front door.

Chloe is still examining me, her empty blue eyes moving up and down my body. "It's so bright . . . like a sun."

Avery snorts. "Or like a pumpkin."

Chloe shakes her head. "Oh no, Avery. It's too early for Halloween. It's not even September yet."

What an idiot. I'm not even sure if she's realized what she just said to me. But Avery does. Avery is glaring at me, a cold smirk etched between those freakishly large dimples.

I'm busting to say something, to do something, but I'm frozen, even as I walk toward the door. I've never stood up to these bitches. I just let them get to me, over and over. Liss tells me I need to stand up for myself. She's better at this stuff. She's good at knowing exactly how to respond at exactly the right time. But I never know what to say.

My mom used to tell me to just stay away from them. She'd say there were thousands of kids in my school, a whole surrounding city to get lost in. But it's not like that. We've all been in the same class forever, most of us from first grade. We picked up a few kids from other feeder schools, but for the most part, we've been stuck together, the same pre-AP group moved into the same AP group. In some other time-space dimension, we were all friends once, chasing one another, the boys snapping our bras and us giggling back. Then we split up into various subgroups: the nerdherd, the hippie wannabes, the emos, and, of course, worst of all: the richy-bitchies. They watched me go from the cute, chubby-cheeked pigtailed six-year-old to the not-so-cute, chubby-cheeked over-permed sixth grader, to the beyond-any-possibility-of-cute, obviously overweight seventeen-year-old. So where did I end up in all of this? With Liss, in No-Woman's-Land. The history is there, and it's hard to ignore.

"Well, it's a cute dress, anyway." Avery broadens her fake smile. "It just would look better on *me,* that's all."

I stop in my path. What a bitch. I feel the tears start to well. I can't cry. I just can't. Not now. Not in front of them. Not today.

I hear a voice call out from ahead: "Hey, Avery, nice camel toe."

Liss. My savior. She's walking toward us, away from the school. For me.

Avery looks down at her crotch, horrified.

"Hey, Chloe," Liss continues. "Did you finally get that nose job this summer?"

Chloe's eyes widen in terror. "Well, no! What makes you think—"

"Oh, too bad. Maybe next summer," Liss says. "It'll look nice on you. Once you get it smaller, it'll finally fit your beady little eyes."

Chloe grabs her face.

Liss locks elbows with me and pulls me toward the front door, leaving Avery and Chloe to examine themselves with their camera phones.

"I love the dress," she says, whisking me forward.

"Not too fast," I whisper. "The shoes. They're more excruciating than Avery Trenholm's hideous voice."

The last bell rings. We've made it.

I've been assigned Locker #13. Well, that can't be good.

Sorry, I forgot: positive thoughts.

I look around. We're in a new section, the senior floor up top, but it's all the same faces, just a little bit older, a little less pimply. Everyone's scrambling to jam their shit into their lockers. Liss is way down the hall, Locker #47.

Okay. Think, Georgia, think. Be brave.

And then I see it. Positive Thought #3: Daniel Antell. There he is. Cute Daniel. Tall Daniel. Totally sexy Daniel with those übersharp scapulae (oh, what a back) and that thick, slightly mussed-up hair. Daniel, who I've been staring at for three years, who trips me up every time we talk (we've had all of three conversations); his smiling eyes fixate on me, and the words in my brain become a jumbled mess. All otherwise intelligent, organized thoughts crumble in his presence.

He's at Locker #10.

Three doors down.

So close to me.

He sees that I'm staring at him, so he smiles and waves. And what's the first thing I do? I look down, at my schedule. (Smile back, damn it!)

I force myself to look back up at him, and I muster out a "Hey."

That's it. Just "Hey."

"What's your schedule?"

I look behind me. He must be talking to someone else. Only quiet Steve Westerman is there, and he's busy overthinking the organization of his one-foot-by-five-foot locker space.

I look back at Daniel. "Oh, um . . . Let's see." I fumble with my schedule. "Um, AP history, with Springfield—that should be fun; chem, with that nut-job Zittel . . ."

"Oh yeah, they call him Zitzoid. Good luck with that."

Daniel's just so nice. He's not part of any subgroup, but instead he navigates them all fluidly. Always has. I mean, he's not especially interested in being part of any one group. And Liss doesn't get why I like him so much. He's too lanky, she says, and too sensitive. She's had a bunch of AP science classes with him and even got to be his lab partner in bio last year. She said he had a hard time during dissection, that he didn't want to be the one to cut open the frog. I don't know why that's so bad (I couldn't have done it, either), but she says she just can't think of him as anything more than a brother. If only that were my problem, I could talk to him like a normal person.

"Thanks," I force out. "I'll need it."

He walks to my locker and looks over my shoulder to read my schedule. "What else you got?" I can smell him. Like pine or rosemary or some dark scent.

"What's the rest of your schedule?" he asks me again. But I'm solid stone. No, really, I've turned to actual granite. I'm a boulder in a giant orange dress. My legs are heavy, my shoulders heavy, my blood heavy, and everything is still. Except that I can feel the pounding of my heart inside my brain. I hope he doesn't hear it, too.

He takes the paper from my shaking hand and reads it aloud: "Let's see there. Oh, cool, AP English with Langer, math with Keynes, and art with Marquez. I'm taking art too." (*Swooon.*) "And I had Keynes last year."

I force out actual human words spoken in English (though they come out sounding more like mouse squeaks). "Is she hard?"

"Yeah. A total hard-ass. And nuts, too. She stands outside the classroom during quizzes with one of those little dental mirrors and pokes it around the corner to see if we're cheating."

He laughs. Those eyes. Those smiley, half-moon, beautifully creased, kindest-eyes-I've-ever-seen. Oh God. Stomach. In. Knots. Mouth. Frozen. Cannot. Speak.

I move my lips into a smile. At least it feels like a smile. I wish I weren't frozen. Then I could laugh, too. A nice, hearty human laugh.

He breaks what has now become the Most Awkward

Silence Ever. "But that's cool, you know. It looks like we
have one class together. I heard Marquez is cool."

I nod.

"So I'll see you fifth period, then." He shrugs and hands
me the schedule. His fingers graze mine.

Yes. Yes, yes, yes. So many yeses.

"Uh-huh. For sure," I muster out. "See you then."

And then he's gone.

Shit. Now what.

Okay, Georgia: Courage, like Mom said.

Here goes. Positive Thought #4: I didn't crumble into
a million grains of sand when his skin touched mine. I'm
still alive. I'm breathing. And he talked to me.

And in six hours, I'll be in the same room with him
again. Every day this year. Oh my, I think that just might
be Positive Thought #5.

I slam my empty locker closed and run down the hall
toward Liss. Pumps be damned.

The rest of the day is fairly anticlimactic in contrast with
the First Official Locker Date, which is what Liss and I
will call it forever.

History, decent; chemistry, confounding; English, fun;
and math, I don't remember too well since Keynes spent
the whole time speaking in tongues—sorry, I mean
equations. Art, I also don't remember too well since I
spent the whole time staring at Daniel, who somewhat
unfortunately was seated on the other side of the room,

though the position gave me a perfect view of his sharply chiseled profile. (Siiigh.)

Liss and I meet up outside the gate. They should really pass us through metal detectors as we leave, too. I wonder how many scalpels are stolen from Zitzoid's class each year.

We head over to Ellie's Belly Busters, the sub shop down on Lincoln Avenue that serves the world's best French fries. My mom used to take me here as a kid. It was a secret we kept from my dad since we were technically cheating on our own restaurant. It might have been the only secret she kept from him.

Liss and I score the only front booth. My feet are killing me. I sit down and throw off the pumps. "First day, man." I lather a fry in ketchup.

"What a clusterfuck." Liss digs into the fries. "Only one hundred and sixty-nine more days to go."

"Seriously? I don't think I can hack it. That's just too much torture."

"Well, except for Daniel, right? I mean, that's all kinds of awesome."

"Yeah, sure." I laugh. "If I could actually form some kind of intelligent thought beyond 'uh-huh.' How is it that I'm the daughter of a college instructor?" It's the first time I've mentioned my mom in a while. I know it. Liss knows it. She's always here and never here.

She puts her palm on my hand. "Are you okay?"

"I'm trying to change."

"Change what?"

I wipe my fingers on a napkin and pull my mom's letter from my bag. Even though she wrote plenty of art critiques when she was in grad school, my mom never liked to write anything personal. She saved that for her art.

I hand Liss the worn paper that's covered in my mom's shaky handwriting. "Here. I made her do it those last few weeks. I made her write to me."

Dear Georgia,

You put the pen and paper in my shaking hand and insisted that I write you even though you know how much I hate this kind of thing. You said you want to remember my voice after I'm gone. You left me here in the hospital room, alone with the blaring TV and the nauseating lilies and useless piles of magazines. You're supposed to stay, to be here in case I crash again, in case I go under.

So what can I say to you, my beautiful girl, so that you'll remember me?

Well, first, that I'm sorry. I wish I could have fought harder, for you. I think I'll be able to watch you after I'm gone. I hope so. I've watched you for these sixteen years, and you've filled me with a lifetime of joy.

But as it turns out, a lifetime is way too short.

Just remember that you are my best friend, my most favorite person in the whole wide world. Know that I'm proud of you, just so incredibly proud—of who you are, of who you've become. And don't grieve too long for me. You are young and vibrant and you sparkle with life.

Live it. Do what I never did. I lived life too fearfully,
I think. I gave up a long time ago. Don't live that way.
Go do anything you like—in fact, do everything. Try it
all once.

And when you're out there doing everything, be brave,
and think of me.

Mom

Liss sits back. Tears are running down her cheeks.

She looks at me. "You have to do this."

"Do what?"

"Do everything. Be brave. Just like your mom said. You have to do this. I'll do it with you."

"I don't understand. Do what, exactly?"

"Like a bucket list. A Do Everything Before You Die list."

"Except that I'm not planning on dying."

"No! That's not what I meant." Liss turns red.

"No, I know . . ."

"Shit. I'm sorry. Not at all what I meant." She reaches across the table and places her hand on mine. "I meant like a Do Awesome Stuff list."

I shrug. "There's not much I can do, though. I'm not eighteen. I can't drive. I'm stuck in this forsaken city." *Way to think positive, Georgia.*

"Come on. There's lots you can do." She pulls out her phone and googles bucket lists. Most of them are pretty stupid.

Like:

Kiss in the rain. (Blech.)
Stay up and watch the sunrise. (Seriously?)
Pull an all-nighter. (Lame.)

"Who writes this shit?" Liss laughs. "We can do so much better than any of these."

"Exactly."

We decide that we want more of a Fuck This Dork Shit list.

More of an I Want to Live Life list.

Fearless.

Real.

So I pull out a sheet of paper and start writing.

This is what we draft:

The Do Everything Be Brave List
In no particular order
Dedicated to Diana Askeridis
......(with duly noted feedback from Liss Ehler)

1. I can't run downhill very well.	(Oh, come on, you can do better.)
2. Do a handstand in the middle of the room.	(More.)
3. Jump out a plane.	(Um, like your dad's going to approve?)
4. Trapeze school?	(Aren't you afraid of heights?)

5. *Skinny-dipping.*	*(Yes!)*
6. *Learn how to draw, like Mom.*	*(Love.)*
7. *Try out for cheerleading.*	*(Really?)*
8. *Learn how to fish.*	*(I'll ask my dad.)*
9. *Flambé.*	*(You ask your dad.)*
10. *Tribal dancing.*	*(Hot!)*
11. *Cut class.*	*(No prob.)*
12. *Smoke pot.*	*(No prob.)*
13. *Ask him out.*	*(She smiles.)*
14. *Kiss him.*	*(She smiles again.)*
15. *See what happens from there.*	

I look up from my list. "What about 'Lose weight'?"

"Eh." Liss grabs a handful of fries and stuffs them in her mouth. "You don't really need to be brave to do that."

That's what best friends are for.

I put down the pen.

"I love the dress, by the way," Liss says.

"Thanks. It's the only cute thing I own. I feel like I've set a precedent, though. And now, with this list, I have to live up to a certain standard, you know?"

"Oh, absolutely," Liss replies, munching on fries.

"So what the hell am I going to wear tomorrow?"

"Hm, well, nothing involving drapes." Liss smiles.

"Yeah, well, there's not much else, then." I think about the remaining two outfits hanging on my closet door: black and boring. "And I have, like, fifty dollars left over from working for my dad this summer."

Liss licks the salt off a fry and throws it back in the basket. "Let's get out of here, shall we? A bit of thrift diving,
perhaps?"

I nod, and we toss the rest of the fries and head down
to the Salvation Army, where I score a bunch of good stuff
that Liss picked out for me. A sleek pair of dark red jeg-
gings (Power Pants, Liss calls them), three ridiculously
cute (fitted!) shirts, a denim pencil skirt (crazy mustard
yellow), and a green striped shirtdress that I'll cinch with
a belt. All for $48.92. Jackpot.

I absolutely love living in No-Woman's-Land with her.

I head home buoyant. Elated. Ready.

I go to bed early, eager for tomorrow, for whatever
might happen.

This is also what it was like sometimes:

I'd wake to the sounds of beeps and clicks and whirrs,
her dialysis machine churning and sputtering and moving
    the fluids
in and out, in and out,
it would be four A.M. maybe,
or barely dawn, the first light of morning crept in
    through the curtains.
She could only sleep on the couch.
She said the bedroom was too small for that damn giant
    box and the tangled mess of wires.
It stretched from her bloody catheter site
low under the folds of her abdomen.

She would plug in each night,
and try to sleep, though the rhythm of the machine
would keep her awake.
Except sometimes, I'd find her in a rare deep slumber.
I'd crawl on the floor beside her,
trace my fingers through her hair,
lay my head on the pillow next to hers,
and feel her steady breath.

This is what I remember tonight.

2

Welcome to Webster High School Club Week, fall semester. School Spirit, U.S.A. The quad is filled with
fifty-four tables, each one dedicated to Spanish or French
or chess or photography or paintball or premed or fenc-
ing or computers or the earth or films or chemistry or
fashion.

"And out of all this shit, you pick cheer?" Liss elbows
me.

"Haha. Very funny."

"No, seriously, Georgia," Liss says. "Why cheerleading?"

I think of my mom and start to tear up. I shake my
head. I don't want to talk about her right now.

"You're still going to do it, even though Avery and
Chloe are involved?"

"*Especially* because Avery and Chloe are involved."
It's time to face my fears. "Anyway, it's on the list." I

shrug. "And that list is sacred. What are you going to sign up for?"

"Nada, my friend." Liss throws her hands up.

"Do Everything Be Brave, my friend."

"Aw, shit. Fine." We pass by the WHS Go-Karting Club table, and Liss grabs a brochure.

"Go-karting? Seriously?"

Liss smiles. She *would* choose go-karting. I bet she'll even go.

Liss has always been feisty and unpredictable. When I first met her, she had supershort fire-red hair. We were only in the eighth grade, but she would wear bright red lipstick, and her translucent skin was thick with powder. She was almost as thin as Avery Trenholm but much more badass and unforgiving. She refused to play the game, to follow the pack of animals.

When she first transferred from the suburbs, we didn't speak for the entire year. I was somewhat of a loner, trying my darndest to be nice to everyone but friends with no one in particular, and she was new and messy and bow-legged and she limps a little when she walks for no other reason except that it's how she was made, and it was reason enough to displace her in No-Woman's-Land with me. That, and perhaps her choice.

But the last week of June, we somehow ended up walking the parameter of the playground every day for the fifty minutes of lunch, munching on our sandwiches and dropping crumbs for the birds and the squirrels. We bonded over music and movies and TV and whatever else mat-

tered most that year. We confided our life stories. She told
me that her parents divorced when she was five. When
they fell in love they were both free-spirited potheads,
and Liss was most likely an accidental product of a drug-
induced haze. But then after college, her dad went corporate (tax attorney), and her mom (a medical social
worker) finally drew the line when he bought a BMW.
Liss has since split her weeks between them. She described her parents as young and lenient; I said mine were
older and overprotective. I think we both wanted what
the other had.

We traded numbers and e-mail and ended up spending the whole summer together, my mom carting us
around town, shopping and movies and the beach and
whatever else we wanted. We stayed side by side as much
as possible once we started at Webster, choosing the same
electives and languages (photo, culinary arts, French)
and deciding not to join anything beyond that, until
today.

Bodies swarm around us. "Do you see cheerleading?"
I'm really ready to do this.

"No . . ." Liss strains her head over the bustling crowd.
Her hair has since grown out past her shoulders, and today
it's tied in two French braids with wisps escaping in every direction. "But I see Soccer Club."

"They have a club? Aren't they just a team?"

"Technicalities, my friend. I think they're like fans,
not players. Anyway, what I *do* know"—she eyes the
members—"is that they are some of the most scrumptious

young men. And it looks like they've all been caught in one net. Rawr."

"Eh. They're okay. . . ."

"What? Okay? Come on, let's go over there. Look at them. They're really hot. Like all of them."

"They're no Daniel Antell. . . ."

"You're obsessed."

"You go. I'll meet up with you. I want to find the cheerleading squad."

"Okay, but be careful out there."

I make my way through the traffic down to where Avery is sitting in her tiny little skirt surrounded by other tiny skirts. I stop at the Earth Club table two doors down and pretend to read a pamphlet about global warming. I spy the cheer table. A gaggle of skirts are all smiling coldly at the passing crowd, with Avery Trenholm leading the brigade. What *am* I doing?

I have a plan, though. I'm going to be the most real cheerleader they've ever seen. I'm going to draw energy from my mom, and I'm going to smile and trust and beam with as much joy as I can muster, just like she used to do.

And I'm going to do a cartwheel.

I love cartwheels. I love the sensation of hurtling through the air, upside down, an unstoppable wheelbarrow of motion, armslegsfeet out of control, defying gravity, if ever so briefly, blood tossed through veins, a shock to the heart.

When I was twelve, I made the commitment to do one

cartwheel every day for a year. It was part of my very first diet plan. I took the Special K Challenge: Eat Special K for breakfast, Special K for lunch, and a low-fat dinner. They said: Lose six pounds in two weeks! I figured if I could quadruple it, I could lose twenty-four pounds in eight weeks. Plus, I decided to start running. And do a cartwheel every day for a year.

Needless to say, I lost the cereal challenge, but not the weight. (And I lasted only four days. I was freakin' hungry.) After pulling my hamstrings during my one wild attempt to be a marathoner, I made a new commitment to run only if being chased by a bear or some other frothing wild animal. However, I'm extremely proud to say that I kept my promise to the cartwheel.

I can still do it, even today. And a round-off. There's a tiny courtyard behind our apartment building where there's just enough room for one full gymnastic move. Every few days, I hoist my one-hundred-and-blah-de-blah-pound self (the exact number is irrelevant and supersecret) across the concrete.

But really, what I can't say aloud to Liss for fear of breaking down completely is that I want to try cheer first to honor my mom. She used to show me pictures of her with her friends when they were in high school—she said it was the best time of her life. She was actually a cheerleader, which I couldn't believe when she first told me. Last year, when she came home from the hospital after her last stent procedure, we'd flipped through the faded Polaroids and laughed at how short their skirts were, how they'd feathered their hair so stiff. She said that even though her best friends were all sizes 4 and 6 (and she clearly wasn't) and that she secretly felt self-conscious most of the time, they still accepted her. They still let her stand in front of the entire school with pom-poms and a short skirt, and she absolutely loved it. She said she loved doing cartwheels every day with people, for people. She loved pumping the crowds with joy and energy.

She talked about everything that came after—how the art world was so tough. How there was no money and little gratification in it. How owning a restaurant with my dad was even harder. She described the miscarriages and endless fertility treatments when she was trying to have me.

She held the photos and said that second to being a mom, this had been the best time of her life.

I like to imagine her that way, how she was long before I was born, before the interminable rejections got to her.

But at the end, she told me to be brave—to try anything and everything.

And now, when I think about it, I think maybe she was the one who was the most confident, even more than her friends. She was the one who demanded attention, and because she never let on that she was secretly nervous, secretly afraid, no one else knew.

I'm going to do my best to demand their attention, to show them what I've got.

I step over to the table.

"Georgia?" Avery looks up from her post, cracks some

gum, and snickers. "Are *you* thinking about trying out for cheer?"

Ugh. I just don't understand. *Why* is she so mean?

"Maybe," I mutter. "Can I? I mean, if I'm a senior?"

Avery's about to say no when Chloe whispers in her ear, "That could work for Junior Varsity. Miss Rawls said we have to, you know, diversify." She's not very good at whispering.

"I don't think she meant *that*. . . ."

"When you say 'that,' you mean my weight, right? You don't think I can be a cheerleader because I'm a senior, or because I'm fat?" The words pour forth from my mouth, but I can't believe it's my voice I hear. Where did that come from?

Chloe's eyes widen. Avery flips her hair and stumbles over her words. "What? No—I didn't mean—"

"You can try out for the Junior Varsity squad," Chloe finally says.

Avery looks away. The last thing she wants is me associating with her circle of friends. Especially after Liss's jab last week. I catch her eye. "Great," I say, as bubbly as ever. I even flip my hair. It's heavy with curls, so it doesn't have quite the same effect as Avery's smooth princess locks. "So when are tryouts?"

"Oh, well, you'll have to dedicate a lot of time and money—" She struggles to find a loophole to keep me from coming.

Chloe interrupts her. "Come to practice next Monday three P.M., and we'll teach you the routines. Tryouts start

Wednesday. You have to sign up for your slot here." Huh. She seems nice enough. Maybe I've been too hard on Chloe. Maybe I have a snowball's chance in hell, after all. She holds out a pen and a clipboard and issues me a gigantic smile. It might even be genuine.

Okay. We've been in the same classes for the last four years and my best friend just did you the honor of insulting your face, but sure, I'll pretend that everything's fine and normal between us. I take the clipboard from her. She hands me a pen.

Avery stands up and walks away.

I write my name. My hand is shaking.

Then she gives me a thick folder full of pages and pages of info, including one particular brochure printed in fluorescent pink that catches my attention:

WEBSTER HIGH SCHOOL
CHEER SQUAD
THERE'S MORE TO CHEER THAN MEETS THE EYE.

REAL-WORLD ADVICE
from one cheerleader to another

BEFORE TRYOUTS:
GET OFF YOUR BUTT
BUILD MUSCLE
STRETCH
TUMBLING
DANCE: JAZZ/HIP-HOP/AEROBICS

Go to ALL practices to learn the routines.
PRACTICE. PRACTICE. PRACTICE.

DAY OF TRYOUTS:
Get plenty of sleep.
EAT breakfast.

AT TRYOUTS:
MINIMUM QUALIFICATIONS
Outgoing, fun, energetic
Think Positive! School Spirit!!
Flips, handsprings, and tucks are not required, but
will earn extra points
#YOLO!

ADVICE
HAVE FUN!!!!
SMILE!!!
DO YOUR BEST!
BE YOURSELF, BUT BETTER!

I muffle a laugh. Whoa. Are they kidding? That's the most bizarre and uneven use of ALL CAPS and exclamation points I've ever seen. Hashtag YOLO? What year is it? Do people even say that anymore? And I don't understand: Smiling seems especially important, but it's only number two on the list. Be yourself, but better? What the hell is that?

"Do you have any questions?" Chloe asks.

"No." I shake my head. "You've been very helpful."
And she has been. Maybe a little too helpful. I tuck the
folder into my bag and scamper away as quickly as possible.

Shit. What have I gotten myself into?

This is what it says:

> DEATH NOTICE
> Diana L. Askeridis, née Melas,
> beloved wife of John Askeridis;
> loving mother of Georgia;
> proud teacher of many dedicated students;
> generous friend.
>
> Eclectic artist,
> Associate Professor of Drawing and Printmaking
>   at Chicago City College,
> co-owner of John's Diner & Family Restaurant
>   in downtown Chicago.
>
> Visitation: Thursday 4 P.M. to 9 P.M.
> at Smith-Corcoran Funeral Home,
> 6150 N. Cicero Ave.,
> Chicago.

This is what it doesn't say:

> Long before it all fell apart,
> on the very last day of summer, the winds hadn't yet turned

but the leaves were dropping and the sun was low in the
 sky.
I had just turned twelve.
She called in to work and pulled me out of school,
and we drove up north
to the nice part of town where the beaches are clean and
 quiet and mostly empty.
We floated in the cold waters of Lake Michigan, pretended
 we were rich, carefree.

She didn't care what other people thought,
how heavy she was, how she looked in her bathing suit,
if she laughed too loudly.

I pretended not to care, too.

She ran to the shallow edge of the beach
and hoisted herself through the air,
a full cartwheel.

She did a full cartwheel at size 24.

She laughed, and I laughed,
and then I applauded.
She was radiant that day.

3

Dad slides my history homework over and places a giant mound of spaghetti and meat sauce in front of me. "There," he says. "Eat."

It's just about the only way he knows how to communicate with me, through food. He kisses the top of my head and walks back to the front to count the register. It's an hour before closing. The restaurant is empty. It's slow tonight. A few regulars pick at their plates, but no one else is coming in.

Then again, it's always slow these days. I guess there was a time, back when I was really little, business was good and my parents actually made a bit of a profit. I vaguely remember taking a few family vacations, down to Florida, out to L.A. for my mom's work, and one big trip when I was six all the way back to Greece, to my father's village. I barely remember it, but from the photos it looks like we were all really happy. My dad was proud to return, a successful American who had enough money to rent a real German Audi and to fold rolls of hundred-dollar bills and sneak them into the pockets of his sister and her children. It didn't last long, though. Times changed, and my dad didn't keep up. The downtown crowd stopped wanting Caesar salads and Reuben sandwiches. Suddenly they liked arugula and grass-fed-beef burgers grown in Montana and flown in on a solar-powered jet or some stupid thing. My mom kept urging my dad to update the menu, to paint the place in something other than burgundy, to give it a new look. "Brighten up the place. Put in wood tables. Make it so that people want to come in."

"Good food," my dad would counter. "That is all that should matter."

And for a few customers, he was right. He continues to do a decent lunch since he does have a prime location—near State and Kinzie—and it's still enough to make ends meet. But dinnertime is always empty. Prospective customers head down the street to the newer cafés and bars, all with hip, idiotic names like the Hog Trough (slow-smoked ribs) and Green Pastures (build your own salad). I spent all summer working the register so my dad could save a few bucks and I'd have something to do. And I've promised to be here on Saturdays, A) to help my dad, and B) to earn some extra cash. It's an easy job since it rarely gets busy. I mostly just sit at the register and read.

Now that school's started, I still come here after school instead of home. It's partly to keep him company and mostly to avoid being in an empty apartment staring at

my mom's paintings that fill up the place. Tonight, I also
need to talk to him about getting some extra money for
cheerleading. If I make it—I mean *when* I make it (Think
Positive!)—I'll need some cash for uniforms and trips.
The packet said they'll provide funding to those in need,
but I'll still need to pay for part of it.

I take out my homework and the cheers that I have to
practice for next week while I eat. I wind a few strands
of spaghetti around a fork and slurp it up. It's so good,
better than most places. I can taste my dad's secret ingre-
dient: cinnamon. He cooks all the food himself. He opens
early at six A.M, closes at seven P.M., and manages and
cooks all day long. My mom used to call him a work-
horse. I said he was a control freak.

"Nancy," my dad calls out to the only other person
working tonight, "why don't you just go home now?
Georgia and I, we can take care of somebody if they
come in." Nancy is his most dedicated server, who's been
working for him for more than twenty years. She and my
mom were about the same age, and they always got along
well. Nancy sat with my mom at the hospital at the end.

Nancy unties her apron, packs up her stuff, and starts
to head out. "Thanks, boss," she says to my dad. Then she
turns to me. "You take good care of him, okay?"

I nod and turn my attention back to my spaghetti and
homework. Revolutionary War. Second Continental Congress. Thomas Paine. Declaration of Independence. Then
I pull out the packet of cheers and practice under my
breath. Memorize, memorize, memorize.

My dad stops his counting and looks at me. "Tell me some news. Tell me what you learned today."

This is something my dad has said nearly every day since I was in kindergarten. It might partly be a way for him to try to connect with me, but I think it's also a way for him to learn, since he stopped going to school in the eighth grade. He's actually really smart, but he never had a chance to prove it.

"Um, well . . ." I put down the cheers and slide my history book back in front of me. "Now we're learning about the making of America, like Thomas Jefferson and Benjamin Franklin and all of that."

My dad shuffles a few bills on the glass counter. "I remember, from my citizenship tests way back." He takes a hundred-dollar bill from the pile of money and holds it up. "Look, I have one of Franklin. Only one, though." He shakes his head. "It used to be that we'd have at least nine of these come in every day. . . .

"Anyway." He catches himself and lays the lone paper in its own stack. "Benjamin Franklin. He was a good man. Did you know he spoke Greek? I bet your teacher doesn't know that. And he wanted Greek to be the official language of the United States. If he had it his way, we'd all be speaking Greek and then you and I could understand each other."

I act surprised, like I didn't know that, but the truth is he's told me this before, a few times probably. The thing is, though, it's a myth. I looked it up online. I wanted to

be certain of my facts before I went up to any history
teacher with unconfirmed stories from the Greek imagination. Turns out Benjamin Franklin did not want Greek.
A few Brit haters wanted anything other than English,
and they did propose Greek or Hebrew since it was considered to be the language of God, but it was never a true
possibility. And it certainly wasn't wanted by any of the
major leaders like Franklin.

But who am I to burst my dad's bubble?

"What else?" He writes a number and looks at me.
"Tell me something else about school. About what you're
doing."

I take this as a window of opportunity. "Well, I'm
learning my cheers. I mean, I'm trying out for cheerleading."

"Yes? Ra–ra–shish–boom–ba and all that?" In his very
thick Greek accent, it comes out sounding like something
in Greek, with his rolling R's and heavy B's. He presses a
few buttons on the register and it spits out a reading of
totals. He squints over it. "Well, very nice. And you'll
wear something colorful?"

This has always been a point of contention for my dad
and me. He always complained to my mom that I wear
too much black, that I look like I'm going to a funeral
every day, like I'm in mourning. "Who died?" he'd say.
"I feel like I should put an armband on or something."

The weird thing is he hasn't said anything about my
new clothes, about the fact that I haven't worn anything

black for over two weeks. And that of all the times when technically, according to Greek custom, I *should* be wearing black—right after my mom died—I don't. That's my dad. He wears blinders and sees only what he wants to see.

"Yes," I concede. "Yellow and blue. The school colors. The thing is, though, Dad, I'm going to need some money for uniforms and trips and stuff."

He looks up from his totals. Maybe this wasn't the best time to bring up money. Or maybe, with all that cash in front of him, he'll just hand me a few bills and call it a day.

"But you don't know if you got in yet, right?"

Thanks for the vote of confidence, Dad. I don't say this.

"No, I don't." *But I'm trying to think positive, damn it. I'm trying to plan for the best possible outcome.* I don't say this, either.

"Well, *siga, siga,*" he says in thick Greek. "*Siga ta lax-ana.*"

"Dad . . ." I sigh. "I don't know what that means."

"Slowly the vegetables, you know? You cook them too quickly and they will burn."

"Um, yeah, I still don't get it."

My dad and I speak different languages. And I don't just mean the fact that I hardly speak any Greek, while he speaks some obscure form of Americanized Greeknglish that involves a thick accent and a confusion of clichés and proverbs. I mean that if we were a radio, I'd be tuned at 93.1 FM and he'd be at something like 1480 AM. We're not even on the same dial. We're both in the same room, but our signals rarely cross.

"This is what it means: We'll figure it out when we get there. Take it easy, okay? Each day, each day."

In other words, no.

He goes back to his money and I go back to Thomas Paine and that's the end of that for now. Maybe he's right. First I have to make it through. And before that, I have to "be myself, but better!" for the world of Webster High School.

We close up and drive home in his old beat-up Buick in silence.

The tall lights of the city street flash against the windshield. I press my head against the warm window and look up at the towering buildings. They make me feel so small.

This is what I learned today: Without my mom, I'm pretty much on my own. My dad means well, but he doesn't understand.

He'll never understand.

I sit on the faded wooden bench in the locker room, counting the minutes on my phone until Doom Time. Excuse me. I mean Happy, Fun, Smiley Time. A group of half-dressed freshman girls swarm around me. They're petite and bubbly and fidgety and oh-so-overjoyed. They don't seem to notice the thick grime of dirt caked on our neglected lockers or the pungent scent of chlorine and toilet water hanging in the air. They're too busy squeezing their tiny arms into even tinier sports bras, smearing their eyelids with yellow and blue (Webster HS colors), and dousing themselves in hair spray and body lotion.

Nine minutes. Nine excruciating minutes until I give Avery et al. my very best self.

I throw my phone in my bag and pull out the copies of cheers they gave us last week that we're all supposed to have memorized. I practice under my breath.

> *Hey, hey, hey,*
> *We're Number One*
> *We're the Lions from Webster*
> *Doing it Together*
> *Y'all know that it's true*
> *So everybody fight*
> *for the Yellow and Blue!*

The smarty pants in me wants to stand up during try-outs today and point out the abysmal lack of attention to rhyme and meter. But then I take myself back to the image of being up there, a real, honest-to-goodness cheerleader, smiling and moving and getting a crowd riled up. I actually do respect what they do. I crave their positivity, their energy.

And I think about her letter.

I want this.

"They're all so tiny." Liss sneaks up from behind, pulls on my braid, and gives me a hug. "When did everybody get so small? Don't these girls know how to eat?"

"A friendly face." I hug her back. "Hallelujah."

"How are you feeling?" She whispers this in my ear. Then she speaks more loudly so as to announce her presence to the room, to intimidate the girls. It's what she's good at. "It's like the Land of the Lilliputians in here."

"You're wasting your breath with that reference, my friend."

A passing mini, who is trying to reach her locker, frowns at Liss. "Um, excuse me. I need to get my brush."

"Oh, yeah. I'm in your way. *Excusez-moi, mademoiselle.*" Liss lets her pass and then mouths in a tiny voice to me, *"So little!"*

They are quite small, both in age and in body type, but thankfully, I'm not the biggest one here. There's one other girl who's not a miniature; she's a normal like me. She might actually be a little bigger than me, a size 20, I'd guess, maybe even a 22. But it's clear she's a freshman. She has that typical blank stare of shock combined with fear mixed with absolute ignorance. She's cute, though. She's wearing white Keds, black socks, white leggings, and a shredded black sweatshirt, white bow under her high bun.

Liss catches me eyeing her. "She looks like an Oreo cookie cupcake," she whispers. "Or a zebra on parade."

I can't help laughing, even though I disagree with Liss's snap assessment of her. Liss is being mean, but she's just trying to make me feel better. To lessen the competition. To build me up. "I like her," I say. "I'm rooting for her."

"You would." Liss smiles. She gives me a kiss on the

cheek. " 'Cause you're a good person. Gregg's waiting for me." Gregg's her new soccer beau. Turns out she likes the game. She used to think it was boring, but now she claims that she gets it. She says she likes the tease of the goal, the long drawn-out wait. She says it's like making out. She would know better than me. She's already had a couple of boyfriends—Aaron Sykes for two months freshman year and Paul Licata for all of three months last year. Neither was serious. She calls them "short-term escapades." She went to second base with Paul. (Her: "With a last name like Licata, you know what he's good at . . ." Me: "Ew.") But that's all. Still, she knows way more than me. I haven't had one boyfriend, ever.

"We'll be up in the bleachers. And we'll be rooting for *you*," she says, waving.

The minis all start to flutter toward the gym behind her, and suddenly, I'm alone. I check my phone. Two minutes.

I walk over to the mirror. I smile, a wide, toothy one. I crinkle my eyes to make them look happier. I bob my head side to side in rhythm with the rhymes that are pounding in my head.

I could be a cheerleader. I can do this.

I relax my face, close my eyes, and take a deep breath.

I throw my bag into a locker, roll the lock closed, and head toward the door.

Here we go. Showtime.

The gym is reverberating with heavy bass and the echoes of girls laughing and chanting and already giving it their all. The minis are lined up on a yellow line at the front, a veritable rainbow of fluorescent leggings, all except for my fellow normal, who looks like a deer caught wild-eyed in front of a semi. I run over and stand next to her. I figure she'll be my camouflage.

Avery, Chloe, and a few other cheerleaders are sitting at a table near the bleachers, looking very official with clipboards in hand.

Behind them, I see Liss on the bleachers with Gregg. They wave and throw a thumbs-up my way.

I smile and wave back, but I'm ready to escape out the door.

I can feel the knots. Huge knots. A giant, gnarly, tangled mess in my stomach.

What am I doing here?

Okay, breathe, Georgia. Think.

Positive Thought #6: I'm not a freshman.

Positive Thought #7: I'm not dressed like an Oreo cookie.

Positive Thought #8: I'm taking a line from the cheerleading packet: #YOLO.

Shit. That last one's actually not very positive. It's pretty damn depressing when you take a minute to really think about it.

My nightmarish reverie is interrupted by Avery's shrill voice in a microphone. "Okay, you guys! Let's go! It's time to do this thing!" She instructs us to come up closer to her to another yellow line and to group ourselves according to height. We arrange and rearrange, and I end up at the farthest end. My fellow normal has moved toward the middle, and instead, I'm next to a tall, svelte blonde in lime-green leggings with the word *SASSY* imprinted on her ass.

Chloe instructs us to state our name, our year, and one word to describe us. Because I'm at the end of the line, I'm first. Great.

Deep breath. "Hey, everyone. I'm Georgia—"

"We can't hear you," Avery bellows into the mic. "Speak up, please."

"Sorry!" I yell as loud as I can, but I'm not sure if it's loud enough. "I'm Georgia, I'm a senior, and my word is . . . um, happy!" Oh my God, what a fucking lie. *That's the best you could come up with, Georgia?*

No one says anything, but I see Liss nod and wave and give another thumbs-up (so forced), and Avery moves down the line one by one. Turns out Sassy-pants' name is Audrey, she's a sophomore, and her word is, of course, sassy (she flashes her ass and everyone giggles), and my fellow normal's name is Mary, she's a freshman, and her word is cheerful. *Way to be creative, Mary*, I think. But then again, who am I to talk? I'm the fucking seventh dwarf.

After every girl has given her favorite inane modifier, Avery takes charge again. "Okay, girls! We have three full afternoons of tryouts. Each day, a third of you will be cut. It's going to be intense. It's going to be stressful. But it's also going to be fun, believe you me." She giggles at her own little secret joke, and I'm already annoyed. "So now, to start, we're going to begin with the fun part!

We're going to blast some music, a medley, if you will, and we're going to ask you to just break out, you know, to freestyle it."

I turn to Sassy-pants—excuse me, I mean Audrey. "I'm sorry, what?"

"She wants us to dance," she says, smiling. "It's a test to see if we can just like let loose or whatever."

"Oh." A test. A dance test. A Let Loose test.

Okay, then. I mean, I'm good at tests. I can do this.

I work up my nerve by shaking out my wrists and jumping in place. Chloe walks up to the stereo and presses a button on her iPhone. A lone electronic tune starts low and quickly gains volume, shaking the walls along with the girls around me.

"Oh my God, Taylor Swift! All right!"

Here's the thing. I love to dance. I just don't get to do it that much. Sometimes my parents would take me to huge Greek banquets where I'd get dizzy in the endless circles of dance, but I don't go to school dances or anything. Liss and I did try to go to one freshman year. It was mostly lame—well, except for when it got shut down. That actually turned out to be pretty awesome. We sat on the bleachers for a good hour while the juniors and seniors humped in the middle of the dance floor. And I don't mean figuratively humped. I mean literally, in the true dictionary sense of the word. Humped, as in had sex. (And yes, it's in the dictionary, listed as #4. Slang: vulgar. An act or instance of coitus. And yes, I looked it up.) Mrs. O'Brien, the since-retired math teacher, went to break up the massive swell of kids who were congregated together at the middle of the dance floor. Turned out Tim Johnson had his you-know-what in Maggie Kimmel's you-know-where. Most of the kids in the swarm didn't know what was happening—they were just joining the bumping and grinding bandwagon—but Mrs. O'Brien almost had to get a bucket of water to break apart the act that was occurring at the center of the storm. Not even kidding. Principal Q-tip was called in, and he shut down the dance and everyone booed him.

We ended up out on the curb. We called our parents, but because of Saturday night traffic, it took my mom forty-five minutes to get us, and you should have heard her screaming into the phone that Monday morning. "Nine-thirty P.M. on a Saturday night in the middle of Chicago, you throw underaged, minor *girls* on the street? What are you, fucking insane?" I actually thought she was serious about suing the school, but I soon realized that my parents didn't have enough money to hire a lawyer, and it eventually became one of those crazy stories we told over dinner. I still don't know how it didn't make the news.

All dances were canceled that year and the next, and by the time they reinstated them our junior year, I could really have cared less. Plus my mom wouldn't have let me go, anyway. Even so, Liss and I have spent many a Friday night turning my bedroom into a miniclub with Christmas lights and my blaring speakers. We could dance for hours on my bed. When she was feeling good, my mom would come in sometimes to join us. And she had moves. She mostly loved to listen to the blues and jazz—Nina Simone, Miles Davis, et cetera—but she was also raised on disco, Michael Jackson and Madonna and all that. She was a product of the late seventies and early eighties, after all. I know how to let loose. I learned from the best.

So I hear the music and decide to just do it. Just have fun. Taylor's telling me that it's gonna be all right, and right now, in this moment, I believe her. I throw caution to the wind. I chill. I relax. I move and shake and spin and whirl. Audrey and I are jumping and smiling and I'm waving my arms and shaking my hips. The music changes, first some Beyoncé, then Katy Perry, and Avery's yelling into the microphone, "I want to see your real spirit!" and I'm totally there. I'm dancing, and I'm alive, and this is my time. This is my day.

Well, except maybe it's not. I get cut after the first round. Not after the dancing; I made it through that. But they ask us to show them three cheers and to do a trick if we know any, so I split the V and dotted the I, and I curled the C all the way to T-O-R-Y. I even did a cartwheel *and* a round-off. But it wasn't enough. I was let go. After the first day.

Me and three other girls, all freshmen, are cut. When Avery says their names, she's all nice and friendly and sympathetic, but when she comes to mine, she's cold and bitter. I look up at Liss, but seeing her frown and her hands pressed over her heart almost makes me cry.

After we're all released, I make my way to the locker room, trying not to run to be the first one out of there. The other little freshman girls are devastated and they're all hugging and crying and wiping their running mascara in the mirror. I feel bad for them, too.

I open my locker and pull out my bag. I reach inside, my fingers feeling for my Be Brave Do Everything list. I take out a pen and cross out #7. Try out for cheerleading. Time for something else, I guess.

Liss runs in and wraps her arms around me. "I'm so sorry. That totally sucks. You did great, though. So great."

"Yeah." I sigh, folding up the paper. "I can't believe Oreo Cupcake is still in the running."

"Oh, her. She's related to Avery's number two."

"Who? Chloe?"

"Yeah. Her name's Mary. She's a freshman, and she's Chloe's cousin. Gregg told me. He lives down the street from them."

"Shit. It's totally rigged." Where's the Positive Thought in that?

"I know, right?" Liss says. "She didn't even do a cartwheel or anything."

"And she's just as fat as me. . . ."

"Georgia, you're not fat," Liss chides me, her nostrils flaring, which they do when she's being totally, utterly honest. "So stop it."

"Thanks." I shrug. I change the subject. "Well, I guess that's that."

"Shall we look at the list? Do you have any clue about what's next? There's so much more to do!"

She's right. This was just one stupid idea. I've got like fourteen other stupid ideas left to try. Positive Thought #9.

"Let's do it," I say. I throw my bag over my shoulder and slam my locker shut. "Let's blow this Popsicle stand."

We head out into the city, leaving the herd of artificial perkiness and nepotism behind us.

There's this one painting I love:

It's small and faint and hidden among the others,
she made so many.
She covered our walls, ceiling to floor,
with paintings and drawings
nudes and figures
oils and pastels
circular mounds of golds and greens.
Abstracts—
figurations, she called them—
all of it obscure
and subtle
and profound.
Or at least that's what the pamphlets
at her gallery shows read.

But then there's this one.

She painted it when I was seven.
She said, *Sit there, at the kitchen table,*
and look out the window,
as though you're looking toward the future.
I sat with her for hours,
a little each day for a week,
trying hard not to fidget,
just like she said.
She took her time,
and when she was done,
she didn't like it.

In the painting,
my profile is soft and clear,
my eyes serious and distant.
I was only a child.
I made you look too old, she said.
But she saw something in me,
something no one else ever has.

I'm trying to see it, too.

4

The next day, we cut class. It's the most logical item on the list, and it's by far the easiest to accomplish. Not that I'd ever done it before. I'm too much of a Goody Two-shoes. Well, that, and my mom would have killed me had I cut school and wandered the city without telling her where I was.

And it's not like it's a big deal. We just meet up at the bus stop, and instead of walking south, we walk east, toward the lake. It's a perfect day for a day off, too. Fall is on its way in. It's breezy and clear and beautiful in every way.

"What should we do today?" I feel more buoyant with every step that we take away from Webster.

"I don't know . . . we could do anything, really. Movie, shopping . . ."

"Eh, I don't know," I say. "That sounds so boring."

"Well, what, then? It's your day."

"How about the zoo and a museum? Maybe the Art Institute?"

Liss teases me, "You can take the dork out of the classroom, but you can't take the classroom out of the dork."

"Hey!" I nudge her, but she's right. I'm a big dork. I can't even cut class correctly. What the hell *do* people do when they cut class? They always seem so badass, and now here I am not knowing what to do first.

We end up wandering the streets in the direction of the zoo, looking in the windows of closed shops and trying on sunglasses at CVS. We get hungry, so we duck into a Starbucks for a venti Caramel Frappuccino with extra whipped cream (we split it), a slice of pumpkin bread (for Liss), and a heated chocolate croissant (all mine).

Next stop, Lincoln Park Zoo. It's empty compared with other times I've been here, but then again it's a Thursday morning and they only just opened and the only people interested and/or available to spend hours gazing at gorillas and polar bears are stay-at-home moms, small-town tourists, and wannabe-delinquent teenagers like us.

We park ourselves right near the west entrance at the sea lions, which might be one of my most favorite spots in the entire world. They have these wooden benches stacked like bleachers that rise up and look out over the blue pool of water where the sea lions just swim and swim and swim. Their sleek bullet bodies speed underwater in smooth circles around the perimeter of the pool. And then, once they've had enough, they hoist themselves onto a rock, and suddenly they're heavy and solid, a thick mass of blubber and muscle baking in the sun. They wiggle and writhe awkwardly. In those moments, they're almost human. And then, when they've had enough, they're underwater again, all grace and beauty. I could watch them for hours. It's what my mom called meditative.

"You can cross something off your list now." Liss takes a sip of the Frappuccino and then hands it to me. "Like for real."

"But we're going to do this again, right?" I open the lid and lick off some whipped cream. "I mean, if we don't get caught."

"We're not going to get caught. And *yes,* we'll do this again."

"Okay, cool." I hand the Frappuccino back to Liss, take out the list, and cross out #11. Cut class. "But why do I feel like I haven't actually accomplished something? All we did was walk down the street. And even if we get caught, so what? I want to *do* something."

"Well, let's look at that list again."

I hand it to Liss and she rereads it and then bites her nails while she tries to devise a plan for our next step.

I stare out at the sea lions. One is rubbing his back against the rocks like a giant cat. He rolls over and exhales onto his belly. He blows a big sigh out his nose. What a life. Not a care in the world. Oh, to be so lucky.

And then, I feel someone staring at me. You know that

feeling, like a tiny little spider is crawling up your neck? I look behind me, and lo and behold, someone *is* staring at me. A girl my age with long, black dreads, ripped tights, and big ol' combat boots. Her big brown eyes are locked on me, and even though I sort of frown at her to make her stop staring, she doesn't stop. Instead, she smiles.

I turn my gaze back to the sea lions. "Freakazoid warning," I mutter to Liss. "Upper bleachers, three o'clock."

Liss snaps her neck to look at her. Then she hurtles back around and pretends to point at the sea lion, who has now made his way back into the water. "I know her," she whispers. "That's Baseline Evelyn. She just moved here. She goes to Webster."

"Wait. How do you know her?" I whisper back. "And what does that mean? Why 'baseline'?"

"We have PE together. And 'baseline' because she has to take drug tests every month to prove to her parents that she hasn't used."

"Shit." I take a bite of my croissant. "And I thought I had problems."

"Could be your entry into item number twelve." Liss shrugs, slurping up some more Frappuccino.

"Hm. Indeed."

I look back over my shoulder. Evelyn's still staring, but now she's also pulled out a pack of cigarettes, and she's pounding them rhythmically into her fist, waiting for me to do something.

So I do something. I wave.

"What are you doing?" Liss asks.

Before I can answer, Evelyn has dropped her cigarettes in her bag and is stepping down across the benches toward us and sits down next to me. "The sea lions are nice, right?"

"Um, yeah," I agree, not knowing what else to say.

"You're Evelyn, right?" Liss puts her hand out. "We have gym together. This is Georgia."

Evelyn takes her hand and shakes it and then nods at me. "I followed you here, you know."

I laugh and Liss laughs and Evelyn laughs, but I'm not sure she knows what she's laughing about. I know that I'm laughing because that's just fucking weird.

"Um, okay," I say. "All the way from Webster?"

"No. I spotted you at CVS. Then I followed you to Starbucks. Then I followed you here."

"Why'd you follow us?"

"Why not? Had nothing else to do. I mean, you two look cool, I guess. And it was obvious you weren't going to school today. But it was a little too obvious." Whoa, this one's honest. "You look like a couple of convicted outlaws, looking over your shoulders every two minutes."

"What? Us?" Liss pretends she's offended. "No way!"

"Really?" I am actually offended. "It's that obvious?"

"Yes, it is that obvious." She puts her hand into her bag and pulls out a pair of brand-new sunglasses. "Oh, and I got you these." She hands them to Liss.

They're bright red and the tag is still on. "Hey, are these the ones I was trying on at CVS?"

"Yeah, you looked good in them."

"Awesome." Liss rips off the tag. "Thanks!"

"Wait," I say. "Did you steal those?"

"I admit to nothing." She reaches back into her bag, and this time she pulls out a cigarette. "Here, do you want a smoke?"

Liss reaches out to take one even though she doesn't smoke, and the teacher's pet in me yells, *Red light, red light!*

"I've never smoked before," Liss admits.

Evelyn shrugs and lights a cigarette while she speaks. "Whatever. I don't care. There's a first time for everything. Just know that it'll hurt the first time. Like sex. Shit. All good things hurt the first time." She shakes her head and exhales. Plumes of cinnamon-scented smoke swirl around us. "I never realized that before saying it aloud just now. Life. What a fucking joke."

Jesus. Who is this girl? Why did I have to wave her over? Me and my big ideas. "And *ahem,* smoking is not on the list," I mutter to Liss. I try to catch her eye to impart a guilt trip, but she's camouflaged by her brand-new sunglasses.

"What list?" Evelyn says, taking a drag and handing it to Liss. "Is that what you were reading? What kind of list is it? Can I see it?"

Liss sucks on the cigarette and instantly coughs, a low, barking cough like someone's hit her in the chest with their fist. "Shit! Ouch. What is that?"

"Oh, cloves. Yeah, probably should start you on something lighter. But nothing tastes as good as cloves. They're more expensive, but what the hell, you know? I don't buy that much shit, so I splurge on the good stuff."

Evelyn takes the cigarette back from Liss, who's still struggling to catch her breath, and she presses it between her lips, lets it hang there like it's a lollipop. "So, this list? What is it?"

"It's nothing—" I try to say, but Liss interrupts me with the full story.

"It's this thing she's doing—I mean, we're doing—where we try things we haven't done before." Liss reaches out to Evelyn. "Here, let me try the cigarette again."

Evelyn laughs and exhales more smoke. "Like cutting class and smoking?"

"Well, kind of." I shrug. "There's other stuff on there. But, yeah. Just, like, new stuff."

"Well, cool. Let me see the list." Evelyn eyes my bag.

What the hell? I turn to Liss and shake my head. We only just met her. This girl is crossing all kinds of boundaries.

I expect Liss to read the horror in my face, but instead she exclaims, "Show her!"

"What? No, it's personal . . . I mean, I don't want to—"

"Aw, I'm sorry." Evelyn straps her bag over her head and stands up. "I didn't mean to barge in on your day. Shit, I'm sorry. I'll go now—"

"Number twelve," Liss whispers to me. She places the sunglasses on top of her head and catches my eye. She's got that totally honest, optimistic, hopeful Liss grin on, the one that sometimes makes me believe that the world is inherently good and wonderful and rainbows and daisies, the one that makes me expect the best from people.

Shit.

"Okay, fine." I sigh and reach into my bag.

"Really?" Evelyn sits back down. "Cool. Let's see it."

I hand her the list, which she unfolds and scans closely. She places her cigarette on the bench, careful not to drop any ashes on it. "Wow, man. You tried out for cheerleading?" I nod yes, and she asks, "How the hell was that?"

"An unfortunate experience, to say the least," I say. "One that I was more than happy to cross off the list. I am absolutely ready to move on."

"Okay, well, yeah, let's see here. Skinny-dipping, nice. Skydiving, cool. Trapeze? Sure, whatever. And tribal dancing? Fuck, yeah! Totally hot. Can I do that with you guys?"

"Well, um, sure." I turn to Liss, who has reached for the cigarette to take another inhale. She's now simultaneously swallowing down a cough and nodding enthusiastically.

"The more, the merrier," she says with smoke streaming out from her mouth. "Why not?"

"Actually, this shit is kind of awesome. Like, fishing? That's just like, cute, you know? And flambé? What's that?"

"It's where you set food on fire with alcohol to cook it," I say. "The Greeks do it a lot."

"All right! Yeah, I like it. Can I hang out with you guys while you do some of this shit?" Evelyn takes back her cigarette, which is now just a small butt. "I mean, I can easily get you some pot. We could do number twelve this afternoon, if you guys want."

"Um, well, we were thinking about going to the Art Institute . . ." I say.

"Fuck, yeah!" Evelyn gets excited. "I've got some kick-ass brownies back at my place. Edibles are the way to go. Let's get high and go see some art!"

Oh boy. I'm not too sure about this.

Liss is nodding and Evelyn is nodding and I'm just sort of stunned by the sudden turn of events. I wanted this. I asked for this. But to be high in broad daylight on the streets of Chicago? Is this what my mom meant by *do everything*?

"Hey, who's this Diana Askeridis?" Evelyn asks. "Why are you dedicating this to her, anyway?"

"Oh, that's my mom," I mutter. "She died a few months ago."

"Oh, I'm sorry. How'd she die? Like, car accident or something? She was young, right?"

"No." I can't talk about this. Not now. I look at Liss for help.

Liss explains it for me. "She was diabetic and had kidney and heart failure. She was fifty-six." It sounds like a coroner's report.

Evelyn shakes her head. "My condolences. Really. That just sucks big-time."

A security guard who can't be too much older than us jumps up the steps, pointing his finger. "Hey, ladies. You can't smoke here. You should know that. It's a family place."

"Oh fuck, sorry!" Evelyn throws her cigarette on the

ground and digs her heel into it. "Man, you're right. There are like, kids here and shit."

"You could also watch your language." The guard frowns at the dead cigarette. "And don't leave that there."

"Oh, yeah, right. Sorry." Evelyn picks up the crushed butt. She turns to us. "Shall we get out of here, then?"

Evelyn hops down the benches toward the exit. I say a silent good-bye to the sea lions, wishing with every cell of my being that I could be inside the pool with them, swimming in circles, safe and confined, with no opportunities for illicit drugs or other illegal activity to tempt me. Actually, wait a minute. Maybe that's the last thing I should be wishing for.

Liss takes my hand in hers and squeezes it. "You know it's going to be okay," she whispers. "We're just going to have some fun, that's all."

Deep breath, Georgia.

Try it all once, Georgia.

And when you do, think of me.

This is what it was like
at the end, when the sepsis
invaded her brain,
and she didn't make sense anymore.
She spoke of colors and light
and when I told her I got straight A's
she said, *Of course you did, you're in kindergarten,*
they give A's to all the kids.

And then she caught herself and said,
I'm proud of you, honey. You keep working hard, okay?
That last day, when she no longer made sense,
I squeezed her hand and she squeezed it back,
and it was the last day she knew it was me.

The next day she was intubated,
and she hated it, the tubes down her throat,
in her arms,
in her wrists.
She screamed and yelled and ripped them out.

Until finally,
they had to strap her to the bed.

Until finally,
the sedatives wore her down.

Until finally,
she wouldn't wake up.

Until finally,
she was done.

A quiet nurse who was older than my mother
shook her head.
This is usually how it goes, she whispered in a thick foreign
    accent.

The infection goes to the brain, incites the worst kind of
    anger.
And then when it wins,
there is nothing else left.

In the end,
there was nothing left
of her.

Evelyn lives a few blocks away in a small two-bedroom apartment on the twelfth floor of a high-rise that overlooks the city. She tells us that her dad left her mom a long time ago and that they had bought the place long before "everything went to hell and she couldn't afford to move anywhere else. The building's nice, but this apartment's a tiny little shithole."

We head over there so she can grab her "stuff," and she's right. It is a shithole. There's crap everywhere, laundry and dirty dishes and wrinkled magazines from 2004. "My mom's a stewardess, so she's never here." In her room, Evelyn kneels on the floor and reaches underneath an open space of an old wooden cabinet. She pulls out a crumpled paper bag. "She's always on my ass for doing this shit, but she's always getting high, too. My feet just stay on the ground when I do it."

Evelyn stashes the bag in her pocket. "We shouldn't eat these here. We should get to the museum first, otherwise we may never find our way there." She laughs.

"I don't want to get too messed up," Liss says, and I want to hug her. She's just as big a dork as I am.

"Me, neither," I add quickly.

"Oh no?" Evelyn raises her eyebrow and then nods. "That's cool. Just eat one bite, then. You'll be all right."

We leave her apartment and walk over to the 151 bus. It takes us alongside Lake Shore Drive, where people are running and sunbathing on North Street beach, even though it's sixty-five degrees and the middle of September. I guess we're not the only ones cutting today.

The bus stops at the front entrance, where Hare Krishnas are dancing and chanting and jangling their bells between the bronze statues of two lions, who look like they've had enough.

We pay for our tickets and head inside, into the familiar central lobby where school groups and families and tourists shuffle up and down the mass of stairs that weave like a spider's geometric web under the echo of wide arches and towering columns. I'm instantly regretting this idea, not because we're about to get high, but more because I shouldn't be here like this.

This place is sacred.

It's more than a museum.

It's a church.

My mother's church.

She came here at least once each month, with or without my dad and me, and she walked and walked, meditating on the endless lines of art. Except for the day of their wedding, he never forced her to go to his Greek Orthodox church with him (though she did a few times each year), and I think it was because he understood that she didn't need the church's lessons; she had art. She had thousands and thousands of years of human life to meditate on. She had Picasso and Kandinsky. She had the Hindu sculptures of southern India and the Buddhist heads of Thailand. She had Chagall's blue windows and the rows and rows of armor and the fragile glass paperweights.

And now, here I am, about to desecrate her church.

Or am I? *This is what she wanted. This is what she told me to do.*

"You okay, Georgia?" Liss reads me like no one else can.

I nod, and we head downstairs to the bathroom, where we go in the family stall and Evelyn hands us each a piece of brownie. I take one more. Liss takes two.

And then.

And then,

I'm light. And color. And shape. And form.

And I think everyone's looking at me. I think everyone knows.

And maybe they do.

And Picasso's women are thick and round and heavy.

And they're blue, so blue.

And I'm dripping down Pollock's paint.

And I'm a child on Seurat's lawn.

And I'm a dancer at the Moulin Rouge.
And I'm a leaf drowning in Monet's mist.
And Dalí is laughing at me.
And then,
my mother is there,
right there,
lounging in a striped red armchair,
her hips full and round,
her torso thick with color,
her eyes
a confusion of line and sphere,
but tender,
and warm.
They're smiling at me.
They are right there,
so close I can touch them.

The brownies start to wear off. We're leaning against a wall, staring at Chagall's blue window, and I'm exhausted—completely and utterly exhausted. "Can we go lie down somewhere or something?"

Evelyn nods and we follow her down a long back hallway to the new building, where the exit spits us out into the park. We find a tree and collapse under it. Everything is still weirdly bright—the leaves shake in their vivid yellows and oranges—but I can feel the ground, and the earth is there. It's spinning beneath me—I know that, too. But I also know I'm here. Chicago, Illinois. Millennium Park. Georgia Askeridis. Pothead.

"Holy shit, man," Evelyn says. "You guys okay?"

"Oh yeah." Liss takes off the sunglasses, and I realize she might have been wearing them the entire time we were in the museum. She lifts her head off the ground and looks at us. Her eyes are bloodshot. "That was . . . amazing."

Evelyn grins. "Turns out that shit was a little stronger than I'd anticipated. Sorry, guys. Hope you're okay."

She pulls out a clove and lights it. Liss takes a drag, and I reach out for it. I inhale, and it burns—holy shit, does it burn—and I cough a little, but then I try it again a few more times. My brain swims a little more, but it feels good. I lick the cinnamon from my lips and rest my head back on the earth.

We stay there for a while, searching for shapes in the clouds.

"Elephant," Evelyn says.

"Sailboat," I say.

"Turnip," says Liss.

She would see a turnip. This is why we're friends.

It starts to get cold, and we realize we're hungry as all hell. We stop at Dunkin' Donuts, buy a dozen to share, and eat them all the way back home.

I'm not sure exactly what I accomplished today, but I know I feel good.

I know I've done something different.

I'm marking that down as Positive Thought #10.

5

The Second Official Locker Date occurs randomly at the end of the day on Halloween when Daniel looks over at me and says, "Nice costume." I'm wearing an orange shirt with the silhouette of a statue of Athena that I found half price at the Alley, and I'm holding an old book with the words *Forgotten Lore* that I drew on with some calligraphy pens my mom had in a drawer. Oh, and best of all, I'm wearing a raven on top of my head.

Yes, an honest-to-goodness fake blackbird, one of those Styrofoam-bodied things from Michael's that I glued to an old Blackhawks baseball cap. I said I wanted to go bold, but I think today is the day that I've firmly solidified my position in No-Woman's-Land. People have been giving me funny looks all day. But it's Halloween, people! If there's any day to be brave and do everything, today's the day.

Daniel's staring at the top of my head, and I think he

might actually like my costume, but it could be that he's staring because I'm dressed like a total dork. He's dressed normally, a jacket and jeans.

"'Quoth the raven . . .'" Daniel intones in a low voice.

Yes! Except for my nerdy English teacher, Ms. Langer, he's the only one who got it today. Liss thought I was an evil librarian, and Evelyn thought I was a witch.

He's smiling at me. Okay, yeah. He likes it.

"Nevermore," I respond.

"May very well be the best poem ever," he says.

"Agreed! My mom used to read it to me when I was little. That and 'The Bells,' which I thought was hilarious."

"To the tintinnabulation that so musically wells / From the bells, bells, bells, bells, / Bells, bells, bells."

Ah! He's cute *and* smart. "Yes! Exactly!"

"Another great poem. Edgar Allan Poe, man. Nothing like him. How great was it that your mom read those to you?"

And . . . we're having an actual, real, honest-to-goodness conversation that involves something other than stilted salutations.

Be still, my fluttering heart.

He's staring at me, waiting for me to respond.

Right. Words. *Speak, Georgia.*

"Looking at it now, it's kind of sick, actually, that she read 'The Raven' to a little kid, right? I mean, he's freaking being haunted by a bird of death. Way to give a kid nightmares."

Daniel laughs. "Are you headed to the bus stop?"

I nod.

"I'll walk with you."

Siiigh.

"Cool!" I say with maybe a little too much enthusiasm.

We close our lockers and head toward the door. We walk past Liss, who's dressed like Rosie the Riveter. She flexes her biceps and mouths to me, "You can do it!" And then, "Number thirteen!"

Crazy girl. I look at Daniel to see if he saw her.

He didn't. Phew.

We step into the breezy afternoon, passing hordes of people dressed as skeletons and ghouls, farmers and angels, and the ever-predictable guys dressed as cheerleaders and girls dressed as football players. Once we near the edge of the school, I take off my raven hat and tuck it under my arm. We walk toward Lincoln Avenue, past shops and restaurants. It's a perfect autumn day; the sky is bright and the air is cool. The Second Official Locker Date has just evolved into what I will call Our First Semiromantic Stroll. Except that neither of us has said anything in more than a block.

"Weather's changing," I say.

"Yeah," he says. "It's a little chilly."

"But nice," I respond.

Come on, Georgia. You can do better than that.

"Um. No costume for you today?"

He stops right in front of a Starbucks doorway and throws his backpack on the ground. A mom walking out with a stroller and a stressed-out business-looking man have to push past us to walk around. They both grumble, but Daniel stays right where he is. He unzips his jacket and gives me a frown.

He's wearing an orange shirt, kind of like mine, except his says "3.14159265358979323 . . ." with more numbers winding around the front of his chest and under his armpit. Then he pulls his jacket down and spins around. The numbers continue around his back and fade into tiny, tiny font. I offer a silent swoon for this close-up glance at those ridiculously chiseled shoulders.

"Pumpkin pi," I say. "Nice."

"You got it!" He pivots around, a wide smile on his face. "You're one of, like, three people to get it!"

Yes! Go, me!

"Well, you're the only one who got mine," I say, pointing to my bird.

"Really?"

"Well, you and Ms. Langer."

"Yeah, she got mine, too."

He zips up his jacket and throws his bag over his shoulder. "Does no one pay attention in class?"

We keep walking, past the overpriced hipster shops and right past my bus stop, but I don't say anything. I'll walk all the way to the Wisconsin border if it means I get to talk to Daniel Antell. "Maybe next time, you should bring actual pie for everyone."

"Yeah, for everyone in the dorm or whatever."

"Oh, right." Only eight more months until we all graduate, and then two more after that, we all disperse across the nation. It all seems so far away and yet so close. "What are your plans for next year?"

"Not sure yet. Somewhere that's not here. I applied to about eight different schools."

"Do you know what you want to study?"

"Yes. Bioengineering so that I can work with three-D medical technology."

"Wow. That's specific."

"Yeah, eventually I want to work as a researcher in the development of human organ printing. My dad has poly-cystic kidney disease."

"What's that?"

"He has cysts that grow on his kidneys," Daniel says. "He needs a transplant, but it's unlikely that he'll get one."

Oh. Wow. Like, really. Wow.

I take a deep breath. "My mom had kidney failure."

"Oh, I didn't realize that," he says. "I mean, I'd heard that she died. I'm really sorry, by the way."

"Thanks." I can feel him looking at me, but I just can't look back. I might start crying, and that would definitely put a damper on this Second Unofficial Date. Instead, I focus on not stepping on the lines in the sidewalk, just like I did when I was a kid.

"I didn't know it was a kidney thing, though."

"Well, that was part of it. She had been diabetic and had all kinds of heart trouble, which messed with her kidneys.

It's what led to the end. She actually got an infection in her catheter site that spread through the rest of her body and finally to her brain."

I haven't talked about this with anyone. I mean, I would e-mail Liss in spurts when it was happening, but I haven't actually articulated the history of how my mom died to anyone else. It's like it just happened yesterday, and yet it's an entirely foreign dimension of existence, me being her daughter, her being alive.

Daniel's looking ahead now, and I'm still avoiding the sidewalk cracks, and we're both walking silently in a strange kind of rhythm, and I think that I've said too much. I'm a downer. I've committed the mortal sin of TMI. I bet he wants to split.

Instead, he says this: "I have a fifty percent chance of getting polycystic disease, too."

"Oh."

"So, part of my desire to go into research is purely self-ish. I want to save my own life. I want to build myself a kidney."

I want to tell him that he's not selfish at all. I want to tell him about the list and how I'm trying to save my own life, too, and how I'm also doing it for my mom, just like he could save his dad's life while he's saving his own. But then I'd have to pull the list out of my pocket and show it to him, and I can't do that because he comprises three of the items.

Instead, I say this: "I know you'll do it."

"Thanks." He nods. "It's hard."

We walk a little bit more, saying nothing. I focus on the cracks in the sidewalk. I don't know what else to say, but I feel like he wants to talk about this. Finally, I ask, "Is he on dialysis?"

"Yeah," he says. "Only for about four months. Was your mom on dialysis, too?"

"Yes. For years. She did it at home while she slept."

He nods. "My dad goes to the center three times a week."

"Do you go with him?"

"I wish I could. He's out in Oregon with my stepmom. Even though he's supposed to watch his blood pressure, I know he doesn't, and my stepmom tries to get him to eat right, but he doesn't listen. She'll serve grilled chicken and kale salad for dinner, and he'll sneak Doritos and beef jerky at night when she's not looking."

"My mom used to sneak ice cream."

"They told him if he doesn't take care of himself, he could die. I mean, they used the big D word. But it's like he doesn't hear them."

"And there's nothing you can say, right?"

"Right," he says. "And I just—I don't want him to die, you know?"

How well I know.

He stops at a corner and turns to me. "How did you handle it—when she died?"

I look at him. How did we get here, from pumpkin pi to dialysis? From colleges to death? What happened to our romantic date?

"I'm sorry. Is that too personal?"

"No," I say. "Not at all. I just have to think about it."

I think about the very end, the letter, her deterioration, everything that we had to decide—everything that *I* had to decide. I'm struggling for the words. I want to tell him, but I don't want to start crying, either.

"Liss told me you and your mom were close."

I nod.

"You don't have to talk about it. I'm sorry."

"No," I say. "I want to. I just have to think for a minute."

We cross the street and walk for another half block in silence. Finally, I take a deep breath. "Look, I could say what everyone tries to say: That it's all going to be okay, that everything will be fine. I'm a realist, and I won't lie to you. It's hard. It's the worst thing in the world. My mom was my best friend, and losing her ripped me apart." I'm trying not to cry. "Before she died, I couldn't imagine how I would ever smile again, or laugh again, without her. When she died, I sunk hard, for a while."

"How'd you get out of it?"

I feel the list in my pocket. "Well, let's just say I made this kind of promise to her, that I would live and be brave and just keep moving forward as much as I can."

"I wish I could get him to be brave."

I shake my head. "You can't control him. You can't change him."

We keep walking. It's totally silent and weird between

us now, and I feel like that's the absolute worst thing I could have said to him. Shit.

"I'm sorry," I say. "I didn't mean that. I don't know your dad. I shouldn't have said anything."

"No," he says. "You're right. I need to hear it. No one else in my life really knows what it's like, having a parent who's really sick. It's good to talk to you about it. Thanks."

Okay, phew.

I can feel it. Now's the time to do it. Now's the time to ask him out: #13.

Then, before I can muster the words, he points across the street. "Well, here's my train. I have to get to work. Where are you headed?"

Oh, right. Where am I headed? Anywhere, as long as it meant being with you. *Say it, Georgia.*

Be brave.

#13.

Instead, I consult my mental map and construct a quick lie. "I have to go to the library."

"Isn't that like, eight blocks down? You're not taking the bus?"

"Yeah, no . . ." I stumble over my words. "It's a beautiful day. I like to walk." Especially when I'm dressed like a dead, neurotic poet and am carrying a fake bird.

"Okay, then. Well, it was nice talking to you." He says this formally, and he puts out his hand like we've just finished a job interview.

#13. Ask him out.

Georgia: Ask. Him. Out.

I chicken out, though. I ignore my promise to my mom. I put my sweaty hand in his.

"I suspect I'll see you tomorrow in Marquez's class," he says to me, shaking my hand, "if not before."

"Yes." I nod. "I suspect that's true."

And then he leaves. He walks up the steps to the El and disappears in the throngs of people.

I walk for another two blocks toward the library, and then I duck into a McDonald's for about ten minutes, just in case he happened to be watching where I was headed.

I wish.

I order a hot-fudge sundae, extra nuts, collapse into a booth, and take out my phone.

Liss has texted about fourteen times:

so?
so?
so?
so?
update?
call me?
didja do it?
#13?!
when's the date?
did u kiss him?
tell me u kissed him.
omg, ur kissing him right now, rn't u?
#15! YEAH!

Ugh.

Oh, how I hate to disappoint her. She's so goddamn optimistic.

I text back: *No dice.*

Shit.

I chickened out.

Okay, Georgia. Glass half-full.

Positive Thought #11: Hey, Mom, I'm getting closer.

"We've been missing you these past few weeks, Miss Askeridis. Here one day, gone the next. . . ." Mr. Marquez gives me a knowing wink, like he's been spying on us as we run around town getting high on Evelyn's brownies at the beach and on the Ferris wheel at Navy Pier, or at the top of the Sears Tower and with the languid dolphins at the Shedd Aquarium now that it's started to get cold. He's exaggerating. It's really not a daily thing—once, maybe twice each week at most, usually on Fridays. Turns out it's really easy to cut. I don't know why I was so worried. All I have to do is send an excuse through from Mom's old e-mail to the school secretary. *Not feeling well,* I write. *Abdominal pain,* or *We're taking her to the doctor today.* I just sign my dad's name. He doesn't know any better, and neither do the teachers. But Marquez knows the truth. That man can skim us like we're a bunch of fifth-grade easy readers.

"Yeah, I haven't been feeling too well," I mumble to Marquez as I pull out my sketchbook and markers. "Sorry." And I am sorry, too. Missing Marquez's class is the only part of our expeditions that I regret, and not only because then I don't get to see Daniel on those days. Art is by far my favorite class, and it's helping me achieve #6 on my list.

"Well, you look okay to me."

Ugh. It's probably because I've been losing weight. It turns out that cutting class and getting high is the best diet plan I ever tried—I've lost seven pounds—and it's totally bizarre, because on the days we cut class, we're basically living off of Wendy's and Taco Bell and Frappuccinos. Liss thinks it's all the walking.

"Yeah, well, I've been sick."

"On Fridays only?"

"Yes," I respond coldly.

"Interesting," Marquez grumbles. "Well, at least your projects are getting done, so who am I to complain?" He shrugs, marks me as here, and continues down the list, calling off names as we all settle into our seats.

I open my sketchbook and leaf through my drawings. Marquez has instructed us to sketch at least five drawings each day—they can be big or small, detailed or not. "The idea," he said, "is to teach your hand how to move. It doesn't matter if you mess up. Your hand will learn and correct the mistakes the next time. Just keep drawing."

That's what my mom used to say when I was little. I remember sitting in the booth with her, trying to draw on the backs of old menus. Even with crayons, she could produce the most amazing art—grapevines and clenched fists and Michigan Avenue night scenes that lit up with her use of something as simple as golden and burnt sienna—and they were so beautiful, they put my rainbows and sunsets to shame. "Don't give up," she'd say. "It takes practice. Keep at it." I'd try, and she'd always say that everything I drew was beautiful, but I thought she was being nice. She'd even try to show me some techniques, but it never looked as good as hers, and by the fifth grade, I gave up. I think I disappointed her. And now I wish I hadn't been so stubborn. I should have paid attention. I should have let her teach me. I should have been willing to learn.

Well, here I am, finally, willing and ready.

My sketchbook is jam-packed with mistakes covered by corrections covered by more mistakes. But as I flip through the pages, almost fifty in total, I see some improvement. What started out as flat interpretations of faces and bowls of fruit that look like they were created by a five-year-old have become somewhat recognizable as representative of real life; the eyes have some shadow and depth to them, the streets show some knowledge of one-point perspective.

And our larger projects—the ones that involve charcoal and pastels and paint—those are getting better, too. My favorite so far has been when Marquez told us to play with geometry and symmetry. He talked about how Picasso was informed by the anarchists of his time. He gave us a quote by one Russian revolutionary, Mikhail Bakunin, who said, "The urge to destroy is also a creative urge." Marquez challenged us "to find the destruction within the creation." I spent hours on that piece, creating what looks like a cracked mirror, with eyes and lips hidden within the lines.

I won't give up this time.

Marquez finishes taking attendance and calls us all to attention. "Everyone ready for Thanksgiving?" Nods and groans ring out in response. "Well, don't be too ready. We still have another week." More groans. "And it's time to think about your final research paper, which will take us all the way to January. We can't just draw silly circles all day. Certainly, the government won't allow it. There must be standards, people! We must prove that we are actually learning something!" Everyone laughs at Marquez's sarcasm.

"No, really, though. Those assholes really do appreciate art." Time for one of Marquez's cynical, curse-laden tangents against the government and all things authoritative. It's amazing we ever get anything done. "They put me here, an art class in the *basement,* where there's no natural light for a budding artist to actually see what they're doing, where we're inundated by fumes from the chem lab next door. I swear, they're trying to asphyxiate me." Marquez points at the door. "If the lack of state funding doesn't kill me, Zittel will." This provokes more chuckles from the amused crowd. Marquez shakes his head and laughs. "But seriously, folks. I do like this assignment. It's a doozy. I'm sure you're going to love it too."

He hands out the guidelines for the assignment: We have

to research a twentieth-century artist—any twentieth-century artist—and then create five pieces of original art inspired by this artist's work and write a seven-page essay to reflect on how the artist's life and work influenced us.

I know immediately who I'm going to research.

Lee Mullican, twentieth-century painter.

Lee Mullican, my mom's favorite artist.

Lee Mullican, her muse, her master, her own personal god.

My mom studied Lee Mullican as part of her doctorate that she was never able to finish, and she chose him as what she called her "primary focus of study and inspiration." Mullican was a hard artist to study in Chicago since he worked in Los Angeles.

There are no Lee Mullicans at the Art Institute of Chicago. To my mom, this was the worst kind of travesty. He died the year I was born and is well-known in certain art circles, I guess, but he never achieved the kind of popularity that my mom thought he deserved. "He was a California artist living in a New York world, but history will speak to his brilliance, his artistry, his individual voice and beauty," she'd say. My mom had been raised in L.A., and I wonder if part of her obsession with his art was his golden suns and love of all things Eastern and hippie. One winter when I was in the fourth grade and she was still working on her dissertation, we flew out to L.A. to see a show of his at the Los Angeles County Museum of Art. We spent the mornings driving in and out of canyons, up and down boulevards, and alongside beaches and foothills with some of my dad's family who lives out there, and then my mom would head to the museum to study the exhibit and work with curators in their library while my dad and I sat by the hotel pool and ordered milk shakes from the bar. She missed L.A., but she said she never wanted to move back. "It's not a city. It's just one massive, throbbing suburb," she said. But I think she missed the colors, the lush gardens and luminous sunsets. "It's still camouflaged as paradise, though," she said, sighing as our plane took off over the ocean. She pressed her forehead against the window and waved a silent good-bye.

On the last day of our trip, she took us to the museum so we could see the exhibit. "You should see it, John," she said. "The way he uses his knife to lift the paint. The movement and light. It's extraordinary. You too, Georgia. Then, you'll understand me."

I wanted to understand her, so I took it seriously. I was only nine, but I walked slowly through the exhibit, examining each painting carefully, trying to see what my mom saw. Maybe I was just too young to have any major revelations, but I did recognize that her own art was clearly influenced by him, all shapes and form and color. She didn't believe in representing real life in her professional work. She was good at it. I mean, she was constantly drawing what was right in front of her. It was kind of an obsession. Our apartment is still littered with tiny sketches of half-eaten apples on napkins and wilting daffodils on crumpled receipts and the mailman's wrinkled face on ripped envelopes. But when it came down to putting oil on canvas, to finalizing her ideas as large permanent pieces, she preferred the abstract. She especially loved painting the female form, but it was always slightly unrecognizable, exaggerated, distorted. She was searching for ideas, she said—and she often quoted Mullican when she said it—for "ideas that went beyond what one saw, beyond form." She was always worried about form.

I raise my hand. "When can we tell you who we want to write about?"

Marquez nods, impressed. "You know already?"

"Well, yeah."

"Way to go, Miss Askeridis. Getting ahead of the bunch. Making up for lost time, making up for the"—he pauses to scan his attendance book—"count them, seven absences in eight weeks!"

Dude, why is he picking on me today? Sometimes his sarcasm is funny, and then suddenly, it's not. It's fucking annoying, to say the least.

I don't want to give him the satisfaction of a response, so I just flip the page of my sketchbook and start drawing some random lines. "Never mind," I mumble.

"You can tell me after class," Marquez says more seriously, retreating a bit on the satire. He seems to feel bad. Well, good, then. He should. I'm a good student. What does he care if I cut a few classes? It's senior year. Isn't that what we're supposed to do?

Marquez changes the subject by turning down the lights and pulling up a PowerPoint on value and proportion, and most everyone spaces out. Through the flashing light of the changing slides, I look over at Daniel, who's taking notes.

Siiigh. He's just so cute.

I think about my list.

#13. Ask him out.

And even worse, #14. Kiss him.

How the hell am I going to do either?

I really haven't made much progress with my list. I tried to do a handstand in the park, but I was high and Liss and Evelyn were laughing and I almost hurt myself trying—I landed on my elbow and nearly twisted my shoulder. I also asked my dad if he could teach me how to flambé, and he said, "Sure, *koúkla,* this weekend, okay?" and then he was too busy at the restaurant, and we never did do it.

I could try again for #13. I mean, we bonded over Poe and pi and terminal diseases.

I could just walk up to him after class, next to our neighboring lockers, before he leaves for lunch, and ask him out.

It shouldn't be so hard.

It's just a question.

"Hey, do you want to catch a movie this weekend?"

Or, "Hey, do you want to get some ice cream this weekend?"

Or, "Hey, how about we go bowling this weekend?"

(Bowling? Ice cream? Really, Georgia? What are you, twelve?)

I'm too busy imagining all the possibilities of where we could go this weekend to realize that I'm still staring at

Daniel, and that now he's staring back at me. Let me repeat: *He's staring back at me.* Shit, shit, shit.

I look away, and then I look back, and he smiles. At me.
So I smile back, and I wave. And he waves back.

Siiigh.

Marquez throws the lights on and tells us to get to
work. I gather my supplies, paint and paper, and continue
working on my current project—my own modern version
of Monet's *Still Life with Chrysanthemums*—but I really
can't concentrate on anything but the fact that Daniel Antell and I exchanged psychic vows of acknowledgment of
mutual existence.

Holy crap.

Maybe today's the day.

Positive Thought #12:

Today's the day to ask Daniel Antell out.

The bell rings. It's time to do this thing.

Marquez yells for us to "be careful out there—it smells
like a rotten egg just dropped out of a flamingo!" I skip
telling him about Lee Mullican and instead run out of
the room after Daniel. I follow him carefully; I'm far
enough away so that he doesn't realize that I'm crazy
stalker girl and close enough so that I don't lose him.

We both approach our lockers and I try to act all normal and casual (whatever that means). I open my locker
and throw my books onto the shelf. I see him out of the
corner of my eye. He's checking his phone. He's putting

away his books. He's checking his wallet. He's shutting his locker. He's turning around. He's walking away—

Shit. *Georgia! Do something!*

"Daniel!"

Who said that?

Oh. I did.

He turns back around.

"Hey, Georgia," he says, walking back toward me. "What's up?"

Um. Um. Um.

"What are you up to now?" I finally spit out. It's the lamest question ever. Not the question I *want* to ask.

"Oh, I didn't eat lunch today, so I'm running over to Ellie's for a quick bite." He throws his backpack over his shoulder. "But then I have to run back to make up a bio lab."

"Oh, cool," I say. Okay, now I know the answer to that. So, what's next?

Daniel breaks the silence. "So, you looked like you know what artist you're going to do for the research thing."

"Oh, yeah, I do."

"Cool . . ." Daniel shrugs and then nods his head. Oh right, he's asking me a question.

"Lee Mullican," I answer quickly. "He was a California artist. My mom loved him."

"Nice. I mean that you're doing something your mom loved." Daniel nods approvingly. "I never heard of him."

"Yeah, not many people have. He's famous, but not that famous."

"You'll have to show me some of his stuff sometime."

Um, YES, OKAY! *How about this weekend?*

"I'd love to," I say, and he nods, and it's so freaking awkward between us—why is it so freaking awkward between us?

I take a deep breath. And then I go for it:

"Hey, what are you up to this weekend? Do you want to catch a movie or something?"

There. I did it. And I'm shaking like a leaf in a tornado. But I did it.

As Evelyn would say, I made #13 my bitch.

"Oh, wow. Man, well. I'd love to, but . . ." Daniel rubs his neck and stumbles over his words. "I can't. I'm going to be out of town, for a whole week, actually. I'm flying out to Oregon tomorrow to be with my dad for Thanksgiving. I won't be around at all next week."

Oh. Right. Oregon. His dad. Out of town. Damn.

"Oh, well, okay." I want to run away—far, far away. "That sounds like fun. I'll see you when you get back, then. Rain check?"

"But we should definitely do it when I get back! Rain check," Daniel quickly adds, repeating my words. But I think he's serious. I think he might mean it.

"Great!" I say a bit too enthusiastically. "That would be really good."

"Well, okay then!" Daniel says, sort of mimicking my

enthusiasm, and I feel like the biggest dork in the world. "Listen, though. I gotta run. I have to get something to eat and then get to Kolton's class, otherwise she's going to give me a zero."

"Yeah, sure. Of course."

"Have a really great Thanksgiving." He turns around and heads toward the door, and I'm no longer a shaking leaf. I'm a frozen mass of stone. What did I just do?

Liss runs up behind me and practically slams me into the locker. *"What did you just do? Tell me you just did number thirteen."*

"I think I just did number thirteen," I respond, shaking myself out of my catatonic state.

"So . . . ?" she says with bated breath.

"Not this weekend. Not next weekend. He's out of town. But in the future, I think," I say. "Definitely, most likely, most probably, sometime in the near distant future. . . ."

"Number thirteen! Number thirteen!" Liss is dancing and screaming this as we make our way toward the door.

I try to shush her, but it's no use. She should have been the one to try out for cheerleading. The girl sure can be enthusiastic when she really wants to be.

I, too, am proud of myself.

I did something other than eat a brownie laced with hallucinogenic substances.

I asked out Daniel Antell.

And he almost said yes.

This is what it was like:

> My mother,
> my father,
> their electric laughter,
> another time,
> another life.

> She saw everything inside his eyes.
> Theirs was a simple love story
> like all the others that have been written.
> That electric something caught them, energy through
>   every cell, a swelling pulse, a heavy throb, burrowed
>   inside the thick muscles of the human heart.

> I think I understand.

> He sits now with a TV that is on, always on,
> his thumb on the arrow, the volume turned up,
> but it can't drown out the echoes of her laughter—
> it doesn't fill the room enough to make it silent inside
>   his head.

6

After school, Liss and Evelyn come with me down to my dad's restaurant. It's a Friday night, but it's slow and so he lets us mess around behind the counter, and we make a ginormous ice-cream sundae: three scoops of choco-late, two scoops of strawberry, one each of vanilla and butter pecan, hot fudge, caramel sauce, extra whipped cream, extra peanuts, and five cherries (one for me, one for Evelyn, and three for Liss), all piled into an extra-large ceramic bowl that's usually reserved for family-sized salads.

We all cozy up in the front booth. "So Georgia Asker-idis asked out Daniel Antell," Evelyn says, taking a big bite of strawberry. "She finally went for it."

"You should have seen her, Evelyn." Liss scoops up a glob of whipped cream. "She was suave. All cute and gig-gly, tilting her head, and being all flirty. It was like she'd done it a thousand times."

"I was not." I shake my head and take a bite of the sundae. The girl exaggerates. "And, not so loud. My dad's right there."

He's only six feet away at the cash register. The last thing I need is for him to hear us. We've never had a direct conversation about it, but I can bet with 100 percent certainty that he would not approve of me even thinking about guys, let alone asking them out. I overheard my mom and dad talking one night down the hall after he became very upset over my obsession with Robert Pattinson in the sixth grade. "What will people say, all this obsessing over a grown man? She's only eleven years old!"

I didn't know what people he was talking about. I didn't know who was watching or even caring about what I did or who I had a crush on. But my mom ignored that part of it: "John, what are you going to do when she actually starts to want to date? Are you going to send her to the convent in the village?" I couldn't hear his response, but I could pretty much guess what it was. A solid yes.

"You were, too." Liss crinkles her nose at me. "You were great."

"So, like, now what?" Evelyn asks, her mouth full of caramel sauce. "Did you set a date for after Thanksgiving or what? What's the plan?"

I shake my head and scrape up some hot fudge. "I have absolutely no idea. I mean, do I wait to ask him again, or do I wait for him to ask me? We didn't really figure out what would happen when or where. It was more of like a sure, maybe, we'll see."

"Well, if I had waited for Gregg to ask me out"—Liss throws a cherry into her mouth—"I'd be single and go-karting right now."

"I think I'll wait. I mean, maybe he was just being nice?"

"Come on, Georgia," Liss says. "Stop that."

"Seriously, though," I say. "Isn't there a fine line be-tween being brave and being a stalker?"

"She's got a point," Evelyn says.

"How's it going with Gregg?" I ask, changing the sub-ject because I'm getting sick of hearing about me, myself, and I. "It's been, what, three months already?"

"That's a record for me, isn't it?" Liss smiles. "It's going *so* well. Like really well. He's just the sweetest guy. Really." The girl is smitten.

"So, dirty details?" Evelyn's obsessed with all things scandalous. At first it was kind of fun, but it's starting to get old fast.

Liss shrugs. "We're taking it slow. You know, slow but steady."

Evelyn rolls a chocolate-covered cherry in her teeth. "Does he, like, you know, enjoy the taste of sweet, young, succulent fruit?" She swallows and licks the front of her teeth. "And yes, I'm talking about oral."

"Uuugghh." Liss and I both groan at the same time. "Evelyn, that's disgusting!" She's freakin' obsessed.

"No! We are not doing anything like *that*!" Liss insists. She changes the subject by shifting her attention back to me. "Anyway, I don't know what to tell you, Georgia. It's not like I really know that much about guys or relationships. What I do know, however, is that we have a list of items to complete. What's next? Trapeze school?"

I dig into my bag and pull out the list, which is now smeared and faded and wrinkled from being folded and unfolded so much. "Hm. Not so much. A) I called, and it's pretty damn expensive, so it'll have to wait until spring when I've saved enough. And B) they're closed for the winter, so . . . it would have to wait until spring regardless."

Liss leans over and rereads the list. "And I assume for the same reason skinny-dipping and fishing are out?"

"Indeed."

"How about the tribal-dancing thing? There's that place by your house that has classes, right? What are you guys doing next Saturday, after Thanksgiving? We could totally do it then . . . ?"

I nod, but Evelyn doesn't respond. She's staring out the window, smiling weirdly at the sky.

Liss nudges her. "Um, earth to Evelyn. Hello? Saturday?"

Evelyn turns to us. "Sorry. What? I didn't hear you. I was listening to the music inside my brain."

Liss laughs, and I try my best to swallow down a smirk. "What song were you listening to, exactly?"

"Oh. It's usually the Beatles. This time it was 'Yellow Submarine.' One of the best."

"Are you ever not high, Evelyn?" Liss asks.

Evelyn's face changes from stoned to serious. "Only when I want to sink into existential loneliness and despair. So yeah, I'm pretty much always high."

Evelyn doesn't talk too much about why she sinks into existential loneliness and despair, but I have a feeling that whatever she's been through hasn't been easy.

"Okay," Liss says. "Well, are you around next Saturday?"

Evelyn shrugs. "It's Thanksgiving weekend, the busiest travel weekend of the year, and my mom's a flight attendant who never takes me anywhere unless it's a permanent move, so what do you think? I'm here. Where else would I be?"

"Me too," I say. "I can get a day off from my dad. It's not like anyone's here on Saturdays, anyway, and Nancy can cover, I think."

"Cool. It's a plan, then," Liss says, scraping the bottom of the bowl. "Next Saturday, we shake our asses to some crazy tribal yoga shit. Perhaps the teacher will be hot and tattooed and have a thing for stretching out hips."

Evelyn licks the front of her teeth again, and Liss and I both groan and feign nausea.

And then we look down at the sundae, which is mostly gone, and the real nausea comes to my throat. We've eaten a good two-thirds of it. I raise a paper napkin in defeat.

"I think I'm gonna be sick." I lean back in the booth. I ate waaay too much.

"I know," Liss says. "They're going to have to charge me for my extra weight when I board the plane." Liss is going to Belize for two weeks over winter break as part of a study abroad program that's open to the top-scoring students in AP biology. She says she doesn't want to major in science, but she's so good, she can't help it. I'm so majorly jealous. She's going to hike through the rain forests of Central America searching for monkeys and pyramids, while I'll be stuck inside an empty apart-ment with five feet of snow piled up at my door. Why did I have to end up in remedial chemistry? The best trip they could offer would be a visit to Marie Curie's grave.

"I feel worse than that time we got those two Party Packs from Taco Bell." Liss laughs and holds her stom-ach. "I thought I felt sick then."

"You were high," Evelyn says. "You couldn't feel any-thing."

"You're probably right." Liss laughs. "That was some good shit that day."

"Shut up, you guys!" I look over at my dad, and he smiles at me. He likes it when I bring my friends to the restaurant. He thinks it means he doesn't have to worry about me, that someone's taking care of me. If only he knew.

He walks over to our table, grabs a clean spoon from a nearby table, and takes a bite of some melting ice-cream salad. "Ah, girls! How delicious! You are all chefs of the very finest quality," he says. "I will hire you tomorrow!"

Liss and Evelyn giggle, smitten by my father's Greek accent.

"So, tell me some news."

"Mr. Askeridis"—Liss leans toward my dad—"how did you and Georgia's mom fall in love? Did you go after her or did she go after you?" She places her chin in her hands like she's five. "Was there passion from the very start?"

I snap a dirty glance at Liss. What is she doing? We don't ask my dad these types of questions. We do not discuss love or dates or anything involving passion. These words do not exist in my father's world.

I want to kill her.

"Well, you know . . ." My dad motions for Liss to move over so he can sit down next to her. "It was like this: It was a blind date. When we met, Diana thought I was too old for her. And I probably was. But, I guess, now that I think about it, I liked her from the very first night. I was working in a grocery store at that time, and we learned this: That she grew up in a grocery store. That's when we knew that age didn't matter. So what I'm saying is, I guess that's when I started."

Liss is stunned into silence, as am I. That's the most I've ever heard my dad say about my mom ever. Not even at the funeral did he talk about her or say much of anything at all.

I can see small tears welling up in the corners of his

eyes, but he blinks to hold them back. "Anyway, girls," my dad continues, his voice a bit hoarse now, "why do you ask? What is this about love? You are too young, I think, maybe, to be asking these questions."

"Certainly not, Mr. Askeridis. We'll be able to vote next year," Liss says. "Soon after is love, marriage, and babies in a carriage!"

I shoot Liss a dirty look. Way to make my already depressed father more neurotic.

"Be careful, girls. *Pnigese s'ena koutali nero,*" my dad says, looking straight at me, as though I know what he's saying. I shake my head, and he translates: "If you're not careful, you'll drown in a spoon of water."

"What the fu—" Evelyn catches herself, thank God. "I mean, like, what exactly is that supposed to mean?"

"It means this, my friend: You make life too complicated, and you'll have nothing but regret. See what you have now, right in front of you. It's all here. Your friends. Ice cream. Hot fudge. You know, just enjoy it. You do not know when it will be gone."

He pats my head gently and then goes back to the register.

"Well, that was uplifting," Evelyn mumbles.

"Sorry about my dad," I say. "He's Greek and likes to get philosophical."

She stares at her half-chewed cherry stem. She's turned serious again. She's far away. "You okay, Evelyn?"

Evelyn doesn't say anything, and I don't push it.

I feel it, too, the weight of my dad's words. The reality of a spoon of water.

Liss catches my eye and smiles, a sad, knowing smile. She understands how much is gone. How much we all miss my mom. How she would have had a different story about how they met. How she would have wanted to know everything about me and Daniel Antell at the locker, about how he looked and what I said. How she would have had my back.

I miss her, Liss mouths to me silently.

I miss her, too.

This is what it was like sometimes:

Me, in the backseat of the old gray Buick,
the Indiana skies blue and bright and filled with clouds.

My parents, up front, laughing—
about what I don't remember.
(I wish I could remember.)

Us, on our way to the farm
to dig our hands into brown American soil
that was not the same as the red Greek soil
that my dad described at length,
repeatedly.
We were on our way to dig up the radishes
and pull at the tomatoes

and bite into the apples
that grew on the family farm
that was built on land
that would never belong to us.

But we were there
on a quiet Sunday morning,
the highway long and clear and ours.

My parents, in love.
Me, safe.

We were there, the three of us,
the hot summer sun,
moving on the earth
together.

Evelyn heads home since her mom's in town for four days straight and is expecting her. ("I hope she doesn't make me pee in that fucking cup again. She's going to be quite disappointed after all that Betty Crocker.") Liss comes back to our apartment with my dad and me to spend the night.

My dad takes a shower and falls asleep on the couch, *Saturday Night Live* droning on the TV, while Liss and I stay up rereading old copies of *Rolling Stone* and *Vogue* and doing our nails on my bed.

"I could really use a smoke." Liss has taken to Evelyn's cloves. I still can't quite stand them. Every time I try to inhale, I feel like I'm going to blow out a lung.

"Let's see . . ." Liss files through my collection of old CDs. "Etta James, Coltrane, the divine Mr. Ray Charles . . ." All of these belonged to my mom. After she died, I took all of her CDs from the living room, along with her old stereo system. Liss continues to browse through the box until she finds one and holds it up. *The Blues.* "This one?"

I nod, so Liss puts it in the stereo and presses play. "What a voice. Your mom knew how to listen to music."

She did. This one in particular was one of my mom's favorites. It's weird, hearing Nina Simone's raspy old voice without also hearing my mom's humming along with it.

"Is this okay?" Liss asks.

"Yeah, of course. I like hearing it." And I do.

Liss folds open one of the *Vogue*s to this somewhat complicated design; it's a reverse French manicure—white polish below, black tips all around. "Want this? I think I could do it for you."

"Sure," I say. Liss is really good at doing hair and nails and makeup. She has this great way of being sort of messy and absolutely stylish all at the same time. She keeps me in check.

"Too bad Daniel won't be in town, though, to see you all vamped up with these sexy nails."

"I know, right?" I spread my fingers out on a towel on the bed, though I'm not sure he'd really care. He doesn't seem like the kind of guy to notice a girl's nails.

Liss bobs her head along with the music, but she's still able to apply polish on my fingers perfectly. I don't know how she does it. It takes a lot of concentration and effort, yet she makes my fingers look exactly like the magazine. It's like a professional is doing it for me. "This is going to look so freakin' chic."

"That looks amazing. I'm never going to make your nails look as good." I can sketch and shade and play with color and light, but this kind of close design on a small canvas requires a kind of patience that I just don't have.

"Eh, I don't care." Liss shrugs and pulls out the top-coat. "You can just paint them blue with a green stripe or something. I'll be happy with whatever."

She finishes up and waves a half-folded *Rolling Stone* over my fingers to help them dry. "Hey . . ." She lowers her voice. "So I'm glad Evelyn couldn't come over to-night."

"Really? Why's that? Sick of hearing about sex and drugs and all of her wondrous escapades?" This comes out a little more sarcastically than I intended. I quickly feel guilty bad-mouthing Evelyn, but then again, we've known her only a few months. And I've also come to discover that I really can take only so much of her, though I haven't hinted at anything to Liss until just now.

"Yeah, well, kind of. I mean, she's fun in small doses. But there's something else—something I wanted to tell you about." Liss is good at not feeding into my negativity. "And I'm only sharing these dirty details with *you* and no one else. . . ." She gives me a sly smile. "But, um, I think I'm going to do it with Gregg."

"Holy shit! Really?" I jump on my knees to give her a hug. "That's crazy big news!"

"Careful!" She nudges me back on the bed. "You'll mess up all my hard work!"

I lean over and turn up the stereo so that Nina Simone can help drown out any possibility of my dad hearing any of this.

"You're such a dork. Your dad can't hear us. He's asleep on the couch."

I ignore her snide comment about my paranoia and re-direct her instead to the important information: "So wait, when? And where?" Of course, I whisper this.

"Well, I'm not exactly sure yet." Liss turns bright red. "The thing is, I know I'm ready, and Gregg, he doesn't want to wait, you know? He doesn't see the point—"

"Wait, what? Are you sure you're ready for this?"

"Yes," Liss insists. "*Yes.* I am. For sure." She's got that look on her face, the one that sees only the best possible outcome. All I can see are acronyms from freshman-year health class: STD, HIV, OB/GYN.

"What's the big rush, though?" I shake my head. "I mean, why all the pressure to have s-e-x with him?" I whisper-spell the word.

"Georgia, you're paranoid. Your dad really can't hear anything. Plus even if he could, he knows how to spell."

"I know. But just tell me. And how do you expect to make this happen? I mean, where?"

"Well, here's the thing." Liss has now taken out the blue

polish and is applying it on her own fingers. She knows better than to trust me. "There's this party—it's the weekend after Thanksgiving break—over at Chloe's house."

"Chloe? Chloe Hollins? The one whose cousin took my spot on the cheer squad?"

"Yes. Now, don't get all judgy and upset." Her fingers are only halfway done, but she twists the polish closed and places it on the side table so she can look at me. "Remember I told you that Gregg lives down the street from them? Chloe and Avery are hosting a big party that weekend. Her parents are going to be in Cabo or something. And it's invitation only. And because Chloe knows Gregg, he's invited, and so am I."

My heart shrivels inside my chest and drops into my abdominal wall. "But I'm not." I lean back against the wall. I want to melt into it. She's deserting me for the richy-bitchies.

"Okay . . ." Liss leans toward me and takes my wrists in her hands. "Here's the thing. I told him I am not—I repeat, am *not*—going to go unless you're invited too. I don't leave No-Woman's-Land without you."

"Thanks," I say. "But you don't have to. I get it. Gregg's your guy. I'd just be a third wheel." And surrounded by a bunch of superficial jerks.

"No. Absolutely not. You are going to be there because Gregg's your friend too." Liss says this as though it's true, but the fact is, besides sitting with them under a tree on the quad while they suck face at lunch, I've never really talked to him. She spends a lot of Saturdays with him after soccer practice while I'm at the restaurant helping my dad. "And you're my friend, and that's all that matters, okay?"

I nod, and I believe her, though my heart is still lodged somewhere near my appendix. I want to be happy for Liss, but it's hard when she spends all her time with Gregg.

And then I realize, she still hasn't told me how this all connects to her having sex. "Wait, so are you going to do it at the party?"

Liss leans back and smiles. "No! Ew! That would be gross and unladylike. However, it just so happens Gregg's parents are also going to be out of town—a conference or something—that very same weekend. And so, we'll have the entire house to ourselves, including, *ahem,* his bedroom."

"And so, you're going to leave me alone at a frat party with Chloe Hollins and Avery Trenholm so you can go canoodle with Gregg at his place?"

"Canoodle? What are you, eighty?" Liss teases. She grabs the bottle of polish to finish her nails. "And, well, yes, I guess. But maybe Daniel will be there. . . ."

"Really? Do you think so? But why would he? He doesn't hang around Chloe and Avery at all."

"No. But he knows Gregg. *And,* he and I have been chatting a bit at the Belize meetings, so I could probably get him in too."

"Wait, what? He's going to Belize too?"

"Yeah, didn't you know? He wants to major in bioengineering, I guess. Champaign is his top choice."

Huh. So this is very good news. Liss and I are both applying to the University of Illinois Urbana–Champaign, which is only two hours south of Chicago—far enough to be away from home, close enough to be not too far away from home. Liss says she wants to major in biology or something like that (though she should study fashion— she's that good), and I wrote "Undeclared—Liberal Arts" as my prospective major. My dad doesn't even know that I'm applying to Champaign, but I'll tell him about it in the spring, if/when I get in. So far, he hasn't really even mentioned college. I think he assumes that I'm going to go to Chicago City College, where my mom taught, before I transfer to a university. I don't have the heart to break it to him yet. That can wait until spring.

So Daniel Antell might be at the party, too. A Positive Thought indeed.

But then again.

Liss is going to be with Daniel in Belize.

Huh.

It shouldn't bother me, but for some reason, it does. Maybe because she hasn't mentioned anything about it until just this moment.

I wave my fingers to help dry them, and I try to pretend like nothing's wrong. "How many people are going from your class?"

"Four, I think. Marcus Garcia, Pete Hammell, Daniel, and me."

Daniel and me. Why does that last part bother me so much?

Okay, Georgia. Don't make this about you. Liss is telling you that she might very well have sex with Gregg. That's big news. That's her news. Focus on that. She has absolutely no interest in Daniel.

"Anyway, you'll come to the party?" Liss goes back to the original point of the conversation. "I figure we can cover for each other. I'll just tell my mom I'm sleeping here, and you can tell your dad that you're at my place."

"Yeah, sure." I shrug. *Be nice, Georgia. Don't be a bitch.* "Thanks for making it a point to include me."

"Of course! Are you kidding? Anyway, I'll need you there for emotional support after. I mean, it's my big night, right?"

Our nails dry and we spend some time online searching for answers to some of Liss's more graphic questions about s-e-x that were either glossed over in health or that were so irrelevant to our experiences that we didn't pay close enough attention to remember the answers. Thanks to Cosmopolitan.com and Yourtango.com I learn quite a bit, but Liss still has all these questions about lubrication and positions that I have no idea about. It all still seems so unbelievable to me. And frankly, it all seems sort of frightening. I'm nowhere near even thinking about anything like what Liss is about to experience. Daniel Antell is a definite maybe, which could mean *something* or it could mean a whole lot of nothing. Maybe he was just being nice. Maybe he actually just blew me off. I mean, we didn't really set a date. I don't say this to Liss—this is the exact opposite of a positive thought—but I can't help but wonder.

We finally pass out sometime around three A.M., Nina Simone on repeat, our nails perfect, and everything else a big unanswered question.

7

Turkey Day. Oak Lawn, Illinois. South Side, Chicago. The Middle of Nowhere, Land of Lawns and Driveways. Ah, the suburbs. I hate them. Even though we're sort of what my mom used to call "isolated" since we're downtown, away from my dad's many cousins and nieces and nephews, I like it better that way. I like the city with its congestion and grime. I like not being involved in the family drama, the politics of it all. I like seeing these people, whose faces I only sort of recognize in my own, only four times per year at baptisms and weddings and funerals. But they're strangers, mostly. I certainly don't speak the same language: Greek mixed with an obsession with all things White Sox and Chicago Bears, sprinkled with a dash of conservative politics and mini-malls.

We've been driving for over an hour to get here. Traffic sucked and conversation was pretty much awkward and stilted and weird during that whole hour, since my dad and I have nothing to say to each other. Dad finds the street (I don't know how, since they all look the same) and parks the Buick in the driveway. Before he gets out, he takes a deep breath and looks at me with a long, deep, serious expression. I'm expecting him to say something about Mom or about the family or about how much holidays suck when someone you loved so much has died, but instead he exhales and says, "You can carry the pies?"

We walk up the steps, and my dad rings the doorbell. The house is big and plain and ugly. Sandy-white bricks, two-car garage, and evergreen bushes perfectly manicured to emulate floating planets. Everything you would have ever wanted in the American dream and more.

My godmother, Maria, answers the bell, and, along with her open arms, I'm immediately drowning in oregano and garlic. Inside, cute toddlers all dolled up in miniature suits and perfect taffeta ruffles run around at my feet. My many, many cousins (second and third), who are a little younger than me and who all hang out together every weekend, congregate in front of the Wii in the living room, yelling and screaming at Zelda or Mario or whoever they're chasing across the screen. Within minutes, I'm worn out by the noise and energy and maybe by the sheer amount of bodies crushed together in this house. Plus I don't have much in common with anyone here. I decide to plant myself at the dining room table next to my dad with the adults.

Thanksgiving in the land of the Greeks means lamb

and pastichio, roasted potatoes and baklava, and the few store-bought pumpkin pies that we brought. When my mom was feeling well, she would cook a traditional American meal just for us—turkey, cranberry sauce, yams with marshmallows, green-bean casserole. But those were her recipes. My dad wouldn't even know where to start, since most of it was sourced from processed crap, and he's too good a cook to make processed crap. Then again, he's not cooking anything this year. Maria is in charge, and we'll probably be sent home with mounds of leftovers, all of it delicious and none of it even remotely reminiscent of Pilgrims or Native Americans or Plymouth Rock or whatever historical myths we're desperate to believe in.

I pick at some lemony potatoes—Maria makes the best in the world, so perfectly crispy and peppered—and I try to decipher the conversation my dad's having with her. I basically flunked out of Greek school in the fifth grade when the teacher, *Kyría* Anna, told my dad, "*Den mathéne típota.*" I guess I had learned enough to know that she'd said, "She won't learn anything." It really wasn't fair since all the other kids had grown up speaking Greek from the moment they'd exited the womb, whereas I hadn't and was trying my best to catch up. My parents pulled me out, anyway, generously blaming *Kyría* Anna for being a bad teacher, and that was the end of my education in the Greek language.

Even so, I remember enough from her lame lessons to piece together conversations, especially since my family speaks a form of Greeknglish that goes something like greekadjective greeknoun englishverb greekpreposition englishnoun, et cetera, et cetera.

I recognize that they're talking about politics (I hear words like Obama, *lepta* [money], *politico* [easy enough], and *economi* [ditto]—I mean, they are Greek words, after all). Then they start to speak recipes. (Food is the international language.) Then I space out for a while and sketch on some napkins with a ballpoint pen that my godmother left behind after she wrote down my father's recipe for some exotic kind of cookie.

Seconds, minutes, hours disappear. I get lost in my drawings of my uncles' faces, their lumpy noses and wrinkled eyes, in the still lifes of pitchers and half-sucked bones, in the geometric forms of a crystal glass.

And then Maria is behind me, her arms tight around my shoulders, her muscular fingers squeezing my jaw. *"Koúkla mou, eísai kaló korítsi."* My doll, she says, you are a good girl.

This is what's most important in Greek–land. That you are a good girl. That you broadcast your goodness to everyone. That everyone will broadcast it for you.

If only she knew.

When I was baptized, she was charged to take care of me, but we rarely see her, just like everyone else. "Everyone's just living their own lives," my mom used to say. I guess she's right. It's not like I ever call her, either.

She releases me and I go back to my drawing, just spacing out. Around me, the table is cleared and desserts are brought out. My little cousins fight over the chocolate-covered cookies. Maria puts a plate of baklava and pumpkin pie in front of me.

I tune back into the conversation while I eat. I sort of figure out that Maria is asking about me (my name sounds like Yeoryia in Greek), and I hear my dad say something about school (*skoleo*) and good (*kalá*).

Then she asks about the restaurant (*estiatório*), and he shakes his head and gets quiet. Maria puts her arm around my dad's shoulder, and I pretend to not understand. I just pick pick pick at the little crumbs of walnuts that fall out of the baklava. I wish I could talk to him about it all, too, but he would never tell me anything. I'm his little girl, his *korítsi*. Sometimes, when we're crossing the street downtown, he reaches for my hand to hold it as though I'm still five.

And then, Maria starts to whisper.

I pick pick pick.

And then, she says something about a *gynaika*. I know this word. It means "woman." And when she says it, she's serious. Secretive. Hopeful.

And then, she says: *"Nomezo"* (I think) *"einai"* (it's) "time" (in English) *"yia gamos"* (for marriage).

Thanks to *Kyría* Anna and my five years of Greek school, I understand this sentence perfectly.

What the fuck?

I look up at my dad, waiting for a protest, for some sort of objection.

What does he do?

He nods.

He fucking nods.

I drop my fork so hard that it knocks everyone at the table into silence, and I keep my stare on my dad. "She wants to set you up?"

Maria looks at me, her face drained of blood. She realizes that I understand way more than she thought (maybe even more than I thought I knew). She gives me this sad and sorry look and then hustles to take dirty plates to the kitchen. She urges the others to follow her, and they all scurry, grabbing half-eaten plates of cookies and cake and pie and sweeping out the little kids from under the table until my dad and I are left in the dining room.

My dad, who is finally clued in to the fact that *I do speak some Greek,* gives me a blank stare.

That's it.

A blank stare.

He can't say no.

He can't deny it.

I start to lose my shit. I can feel it inside, my heart pounding, my head pounding. I'm pissed. Beyond pissed. "Mom's been dead, what, *four* months?" I yell across the table. "And she wants you to get *married* again?" This is bullshit.

"*Georgiamou, óxi,* no." He reaches his hand out to me. "It's not like that. . . ."

"Well, did you tell *her* that?" I point to the kitchen toward Maria, my godmother—the one who stood up at my parents' wedding, who dipped me in holy water under the eyes of a priest and made a sacred promise to watch over me, to take care of me, to provide for me in case my mom and dad were to both die and I was left alone in this world to fend for myself—this woman who breaks this one, sacred promise by offering to play matchmaker when my mom's body is not even cold in the ground.

What the fuck?

I stand up. "Give me the keys to the car," I demand. "I'll wait for you outside."

But he doesn't give me the keys. Instead, he moves his stare to the table.

He can't even look me in the eye.

I run toward the front door and let myself out, slamming it behind me. I walk away from the house. I need to get away. I need to run, to be free of this day that is nothing but bullshit, but I make it only a few houses down before I realize I can't go anywhere. I'm in a fucking suburban nightmare. I plant myself on the curb under a streetlight, where it's cold and bare and quiet. There's nothing here. Nothing. A few trees, a few cars. No horns, no taxis, no sirens. The suburbs. I'm stuck in the fucking suburbs with nowhere to go. If I were downtown, I could walk for miles, but here—here, there's nothing.

Down the street, I hear the door to Maria's house creak open.

I hear my dad say good night to Maria in Greek.

I hear his footsteps coming closer to me.

He sits beside me on the cold cement curb. "Georgia—" He says my name with a heavy Americanized hard G and without the *mou* at the end, without the possessive *my* that he usually uses.

"Your mother was sick for a very long time." He pauses, as if to think about what he wants to say or maybe to give me a chance to agree. I refuse.

"And, you know," he continues, "we made an agreement."

. . .

I refuse to give in to this. I refuse to respond.

. . .

There's nothing but the sound of our breaths.

The streetlight buzzing.

A lone car in the distance.

. . .

The cold November air moves around us, blowing dust and leaves down the barren street.

And then he repeats it again: "We made an agreement," he says.

Fine.

I give in.

"What *exactly* do you mean, 'an agreement'?"

Pause.

Breath.

Buzz.

"She knew she was going to die. She told me to keep on going."

Pause.

Breath.

Buzz.

"To get remarried, when I'm ready."

"Well, are you ready *already*?" I ask this question quickly, but as soon as the words leave me, I know it's a question for which I don't want to know the answer.

I already know the answer.

I'm not.

It's just too damn soon.

"No, *koúkla mou. Óxi*. I am not ready." He inches closer to me. I can tell he's being careful. Like I'm some fragile glass or something. He motions that he wants to wrap his arm around my shoulders. I let him. "But one day, I will be. Not now, but yes, one day."

Shit.

"I loved your mother. She was . . . she was Diana. There will never be anyone else like her." He shakes his head. *"Katálave?"*

He's asking me if I understand.

I force myself to nod, and then I collapse into the crux of his bent arm, his thick coat soft and heavy under my head.

I don't want to admit it, but I do understand completely.

She asked him to be brave, too.

At first, there was just:

Coughing,

Congestion,
Nausea,
Numbness.

The doctor saw:
Creatinine.
Distension.
Hypertension.
Sepsis.

Thick words.
Medical words.
Foreign words.

It was worse than we'd realized.

And then, in the CCU,
that last time:

The glare of the cold white walls
from the long fluorescent bulb
that fell hard against her
gray skin
against the cold metal
and plastic wires.

The mask on her face.
The steady, careful pulse of machines,
monitors,

mechanical boxes that lived for her,
that sustained whatever was left.

Her body was broken.
She was a butchered animal
with her arms limp
and her chest heaving with the push of the machine,
her eyelids shifting,
her feet trembling.
Automatic responses, they're called.

I wonder what was there,
inside,
the moments before her heart stopped.

I wonder if she could hear what I said
how sorry I was,
just so deeply sorry.

8

Saturday morning, 8:15 A.M. It's early, and I was up late writing and painting and watching old reruns of *Phineas and Ferb*. I just want to stay here, under my warm blanket. It's snowing outside. Through my bedroom window, I can see fluffy globs of snow falling onto tree branches. I could stay here for hours watching it. I could drift back into dreamland. It would be so easy.

I'm in no mood to go anywhere or do anything, particularly not anything involving any level of physical activity, but I promised Liss and Evelyn that we'll do another item on the list.

Which means I have to get out of bed.

Ugh. Whose big idea was this?

Oh right. *Mine.*

Item #10: Tribal dancing.

The class starts at nine A.M. sharp.

I gotta get out of bed.

Lord knows how I came to find out about this in the first place. We can thank the Internet gods, I suppose. Them and my mom's cardiologist.

It was a year ago, maybe, the day before my mom's last stent procedure. I was standing in the hallway playing with my phone while Dr. Mehlman, who took care of my mom for more than ten years, talked to her and my dad inside the room. When he came out, he saw me and got quiet. At first he just said, "You can go in now," and I was about to head inside, except that he took my elbow to hold me back. He was tall and lean and had the face of a bird, and he peered at me through his wire glasses and said, "Don't let this happen to you."

I never told my mom or dad, but that night I made a promise with myself and my future children and grand-children to lose weight and start taking care of myself. Of course, I decided to start counting calories, and I went online to find some form of physical exercise that seemed like it might even be a little fun. I bookmarked links to Zumba, cardio ballet, kickboxing, TRX suspension, plyometrics. They all sounded great, but most of them were either really expensive or met only at five in the morning (WTF?), or they looked like they required a level of coordination that I simply did not possess. But along the way, as I clicked from studio to studio on Yelp, I came across this one particular studio (SOUL POWER YOGA, *all caps*) that caught my interest. It was brand-new, less than a mile from my house, and relatively cheap, especially since they offered student discounts with an ID. They had a bunch of different classes, yoga, qigong, et cetera, but the one that stood out to me was the one called "tribal yoga dance." One class was only $12 and, better yet, only $9 with a student ID.

The Soul Power Yoga Web site linked to some videos that previewed what a typical tribal yoga dance class was like. It was *insane*. I recognized some elements from our yoga unit in PE—Downward-Facing Dog and Tree Pose and the like—but then there was this whole other element that was totally raunchy. Their hips were writhing and their hair was spiraling. It was like belly dancing gone wild.

I sent the link to Liss, and she wrote back immediately, *Let's do that.*

And we were going to—I mean, I had this whole plan to lose weight—but then after my mom's last stent, things got worse really quickly, and if I wasn't at school, I was at the hospital and then at rehab and then back at the ICU. I didn't do any of it, and I didn't keep my promise to Dr. Mehlman or to my future progeny or to myself.

I peel myself out of bed and get dressed. My head is throbbing. I pour some lukewarm coffee, snarf down a cold bagel, and head out the door.

I arrive at the building to find that I have to climb two flights of stairs to get to the studio. Liss texts that she and Evelyn are on their way (*Missed the train! Sorry!*), so I head upstairs. By the time I get to the top floor, I'm winded. Isn't that enough of a workout? Now I have to exercise, too?

I walk down the cramped hallway to door #9. I knock first, and no one answers, so I push open the door to a small area stuffed with a couch, a desk, and a coffee table that's serving as the front lobby and three sweaty women who are laughing and chatting it up.

The one sitting at the desk looks up at me. She's young and petite and bright and what my mom would call bushy-tailed.

"I'm here for the nine A.M. class?"

"Hi! Come in! Have a seat," she says. "I'll be with you in a sec."

I file past the two Amazon women in their skintight workout gear and now feel totally schlumpy in mine (gray sweatpants and one of my dad's old undershirts).

Desk Girl hands printouts of the class schedule to the Amazon ladies, who seem to have just finished their class. (7:30 A.M. on a Saturday? They're crazy.) "We have classes for all levels: gentle, basics, power, and tribal."

"What's the tribal class like?" one of the two women ask.

"Oh, that's the most ridiculously intense one we've got." Desk Girl laughs. "It's totally liberating, but it's a workout for sure."

"Isn't that the one I'm here for?" I say.

Desk Girl nods, and they all laugh.

I don't.

It's not too late to leave. I could just stand right up and walk out that door. They'd never know who I was. I seriously consider bolting out the door but then it opens. It's Liss and Evelyn, both out of breath and smiling.

"We made it! We're here for the tribal yoga class!" Liss announces. "Oh, Georgia, you're here already—"

Damn.

Desk Girl says good-bye to the Amazon ladies and checks us in.

"You girls are here to dance?"

Liss and Evelyn respond that we are and I just nod.

"Okay, then. I'm Aspen. Nice to meet you." She shakes our hands formally. "Let's do it."

It's 9:05 already, but it looks like no one else is showing up. She shows us where to put our stuff and where to set up our mats. Thank God it's just the three of us.

Aspen takes off her shirt and pants to reveal a very small sports bra and very, very small black shorts. Like they're so small I can see full-on butt cheeks.

She turns on the stereo and the music blasts a low, heavy bass. The walls shake with the reverberation.

"Before we start, let's warm up a bit. I'll show you some of the basics." She stands in front of me on her mat, places her feet wide apart and spreads her knees, and starts shaking her body, and I swear I can nearly see everything. It's all jiggling and wiggling and quivering. This isn't tribal yoga dancing; it's yoga for wannabe porn stars.

Dear Lord, what have I gotten myself into?

And then she starts "popping" and "bumping" (that's what she calls it) and thrusting her hips and swirling

her arms above her head and her eyes close and she's lost
in her dance. "You want to let yourself go. You want to
let yourself be free. Release your hips, your back, your
shoulders, your chest."

Next to me, Liss and Evelyn are mimicking her moves
awkwardly. All I can do is stand there and gape, but then
Liss punches me in the arm and yells, *"Start moving! Number ten!"*

Aspen shakes herself out of her porn trance and walks
to the corner of the room, where she lights some candles,
closes the curtains, and shuts off the lights. It's enough so
that we can see her, but enough so that we can't see ourselves.

"That should do it," Aspen says, returning to her mat.
"No one here is going to watch you. Just let go. Let yourself be inside your body."

And so I do.

I grind and
I pop and
I thrust and
I shake
my hips.
I twirl and wave and let myself be
free.
I close my eyes.
I bury myself deep.
I bury it all.
I let myself be here,

here.
And
at the end, when Aspen tells us to give thanks
to our bodies,
to my body,
to the blood and
the muscle and
the bone
that moves us forward,
I do give thanks, but then
I cry, too.

It's taken me so very long to get here.

I purchase the introductory package of ten classes for fifty bucks (I want to do that *all of the time*), and then we head back to my place. We spend the afternoon dancing in my room. We just can't stop. The class was too much fun, the music was too good, and I haven't felt this great in so long.

As the afternoon shifts into night, we decide to head over to Evelyn's for the night. I pack up a few things— clean underwear, a toothbrush, my pj's, a change of clothes, and my hair gel—and I leave a note for my dad telling him that I'm spending the night at Liss's. Having never met Evelyn's mom, he'd never approve of my staying at some stranger's house. He's just that archaic.

We walk a few blocks down through the freezing air to the Red Line, where we take the warm train down to Evelyn's apartment. Her mom, as usual, is not home. And her place, as usual, is a total wreck. We stumble over empty plates and shoes and unpacked luggage. "Let's go in my room." We follow her in and sprawl out on her bed, pushing clothes and magazines onto the floor. It's not any cleaner in here, but at least it's a place where we can sit and they can smoke.

We order a pizza and change into our *loungewear,* as Liss calls it.

Evelyn passes around her pack of cigarettes. They're not cloves, so I try to partake. Liss and I each take one, and Evelyn holds out her lighter.

"Thanks," Liss says. "Your mom won't care that you've been smoking in here?"

"Yeah, she'll care." Evelyn inhales and blows the smoke to the side. "But I won't."

It seems as though Evelyn purposely tries to piss off her mom, like most recently, getting caught smoking up in the janitor's closet so that her mom had to reschedule her flights to attend meetings with Principal Q-tip about Evelyn's progress, or lack thereof.

"But one more time, and she said you'd be sent to another school, right?" I cough out. It's getting a little easier, but smoking still burns my lungs and makes me dizzy. "St. Mark's or something?"

"Eh." Evelyn shrugs. "She's said that before, like a million times. It won't happen. You know, we've moved so much for my mom's job that I've been at five different schools in four different cities over the past four years? And I was kicked out of two of those."

I didn't know that.

She reaches out to me for the cigarette. "You guys are like my first real friends."

Oh.

I feel like I should say something in return, something cheesy and heartfelt, something to make up for saying those mean things about her to Liss.

But Evelyn keeps going before I can. "Anyway, my mom's not going to pay fifteen thousand dollars for a snotty Catholic private school that I'll probably get kicked out of. She couldn't afford it."

"Would she move again?" Liss asks.

"Who knows. She might. Her solution to any problem is to run from it."

"What about Choices?" Choices is a city-run school where potheads and pregnant moms often escape to so they can finish up their degree without the scrutiny of fifteen hundred other acne-ridden faces. I guess there are only like one hundred kids at each location.

"Yeah. That would suck, I guess. Or maybe not. It would mean school from eight to twelve and then a job in the afternoon. But really, the only way that would happen is if Q-tip kicks me out. And he's a wimp. He's totally scared of my mom."

That's easy to imagine. Our principal, Mr. McKee, is short and thin and has a bald, shiny head, thus the nickname. His personality is just as limp as a Q-tip, too. I've never met Evelyn's mom, but from the various photos lying around the house, she looks nice enough. After hearing about their constant moves, though, I can see why Evelyn likes to piss her off so much.

"Anyway, let's talk about something else, okay?" Evelyn takes a drag. "Let's focus on the positive."

Ah yes, the positive.

Evelyn unpacks some special dessert for us. We rest our cigarettes in an old bowl on the side table.

"Freshly baked," she says, passing around the plastic bag full of goodies. "Just as you will be in about, oh, twelve minutes."

Man, I love this stuff. I know that this is probably not at all what my mom meant by her final letter, but it just feels so good when I do it. I feel alive. Like really alive.

The sun goes down, and we stay up, stuffing ourselves on pizza and Doritos and Coke and Oreos that are beyond stale but that still, somehow, taste utterly divine.

These brownies are relatively mild compared with some of the crazy stuff Evelyn's gotten for us in the past. I like it. It's a chill night. We listen to music and do each other's hair, and I sketch a bit—images of the skyline, which is gorgeous from Evelyn's twelfth-story window—and we talk about nothing in particular and everything we can think of.

"Hey," Liss says. "You didn't cross off number ten yet."

"Oh yeah," I say. "Right." I reach in my bag, pull out my list, and cross off #10. Tribal dancing. That makes four items out of fifteen accomplished. "I've only completed twenty-five percent of my list. Lame. I sort of feel like I haven't done anything, really."

Liss and Evelyn look over my shoulder at the list.

Evelyn downs her Coke and asks, "What about skinny-dipping?"

"Can't. Already established that. It's November and the lake is a frozen tundra."

"Well, there's a pool upstairs on the top floor." Evelyn checks the time on her phone. "It's two thirty-eight A.M. It's inside, no one is there, and I have a key. This is a no-fail plan."

Liss jumps up and down like a kid on Christmas morning. "Yes! Yes! Yes! Let's do this! Two in one day, Georgia. This is a perfect plan!"

Even in my stoned haze, this plan sounds anything but perfect. "We've been dancing all day and now we're high and stuffed and exhausted," I say. "This is the perfect recipe for a drowning."

"Come on," Liss begs. "You really couldn't ask for better circumstances." Her eyes are totally bloodshot, and she's hyped up on brownies and Coca-Cola.

Ugh. I don't want to get naked in front of anyone, even if it is my two closest friends. The thing is, the two of them are sort of perfectly thin, whereas . . . well, I'm just not.

Whose big idea was this, anyway?

Oh right.

Mine.

It's as though Evelyn can read my mind. "My mom has a closet full of terry-cloth robes stolen from various hotels throughout Europe. We could strip down here, get in our robes, and then all we'd have to do is head up-stairs, tear them off, and jump in."

Well, that certainly makes it sound more enticing. A quick strip, a quick swim, and then I can mark #5 off my list.

"Fine," I say. "Let's do it."

"Yes!" Liss screams. *"Number five, let's go!"* That girl has a set of lungs on her.

"Okay," I say. "But you have to be quiet in the hall-way. People are sleeping."

"Whatever," Evelyn mumbles. "They're dying a slow death, is what they're doing."

Evelyn leads us into her mom's room, which is even messier than hers, and we pillage her closet and each pick out our own robe, mine with a Hilton emblem on it, Ev-elyn's with a W, and Liss's with what might be the Four Seasons. "Your mom actually got to stay in these places?"

"Yeah, a long time ago, when things were better. Now she can't afford to anymore, but she keeps this shit as a reminder of her long-lost glorious youth."

Liss and Evelyn strip down in her mom's room, while I head into the bathroom to change.

"You know we're going to see you naked in about eight minutes!" Liss yells through the locked door, and Eve-lyn snickers. Then I hear them whisper something to each other. Probably something about me.

I take off my shirt and bra, pants and underpants, and I throw them in a pile in the corner of the floor. I look at myself in the mirror. I think of something I heard my mom say once, when I was twelve and I couldn't find a pair of jeans in the Macy's junior department that could fit me. I sat on the floor of the dressing room, sobbing. She had to take me to the adult section, where all I could find were these ugly, old-lady jeans that gave me high waters. I don't know why she didn't just take me to Old Navy or something where things would have been cheaper and cuter and where they actually fit me. I think she just always wanted to treat me well. She wanted me to have nice things even when we couldn't really afford it.

As I was sitting there on that dirty dressing room floor, piles of size 14s, none of which were even remotely close to fitting me, crumpled around me, my mom rubbed my back and said this: "Skinny girls may look good with clothes on, but bigger girls look better naked. Good ol' Auguste knew that."

She was talking about Renoir's nudes, which were always some of her favorite paintings to stare at. She loved their thick curves and full breasts and thighs full of fasciae and muscle and all kinds of fat that poured over their chairs.

I don't necessarily agree with my mom. I think Liss and Evelyn and even the likes of Avery and Chloe all have great bodies, and I would kill to be like them.

But I see Mom's point. I know what she was trying to say.

I look for Renoir's hand in my own body, and I think I see it. A little bit of beauty. Curvature. Fullness.

Abundance. I don't know if I've ever stared at myself naked before, at least not for this long. And not while high.

I look like a woman.

I look like my mother.

"What's going on in there?" Liss knocks at the door. "Are we going, or what? Don't chicken out on us now."

I grab the robe, throw it on, and knot the tie around my waist as tightly as I can. We throw on our shoes and head toward the elevator. The terry cloth is soft on my skin.

The elevator carries us up to the fortieth floor, and my body is weighed down by the quick lift against gravity. Liss and Evelyn both have stupid grins on their faces. They're baked, and so am I, but the realization of what we're about to do has forced my neurosis to creep back in.

"What if someone catches us?"

Liss rolls her eyes. "Relax, Georgia. No one's going to catch us."

"Yeah, but what if they do?"

"Who?" Evelyn says. "The president of the condo association? She's in Maui."

"No, like a security guard or something. The front desk guy. I mean, don't they have cameras?"

"This building's not *that* fancy, Georgia," Evelyn says. "They can't even afford a night security guard."

"Let's just go back downstairs. . . ."

Evelyn walks over to me and takes me by the shoulders.

"Chill out. Seriously. Get back to your happy place. You've entered the crazy paranoid place. I've been there, and it sucks. But you can get out. Make it a choice, okay?"

Liss nods in agreement. "Nothing's going to happen. We're going to swim. That's it. We're not actually doing anything wrong."

Make it a choice.

Easier said than done.

The doors open to an empty hallway. We follow Evelyn toward a locked door. She fumbles with the keys and then pushes open the heavy door to the pool. I know Evelyn says this building isn't that fancy, but this is pretty damn nice. The windows overlook the entire city. The lights twinkle in the night.

Evelyn sets her keys on a table, kicks off her shoes, and throws off her robe. She's naked and slender and very pretty. "Let's do it!" she yells, and then dives in headfirst.

Liss follows her. She throws her clothes next to Evelyn's and dives in. They're both in the water, and from up here at the eight-foot marker, I can see their perky breasts bobbing up and down happily. They look like mermaids.

Now I really don't want to get in. My mom always called her breasts "hangers." They were big, but they hung low. Unfortunately, my genetic expression is a carbon copy of hers.

"Come on!" they yell. "What are you waiting for? Jump in!"

Idon'twanna. Idon'twanna. Idon'twanna.

I don't have to do this. I could just go back downstairs, put on my clothes, and crawl on the couch, go to sleep. I don't have to succumb to the peer pressure.

And then they start chanting, *"Number five. Number five. Number five."*

"Shut up, you guys. You're going to wake up someone!"

"Well, if you don't get in"—Liss twirls in the water—"we're going to yell even louder."

And so Evelyn does. *"Number five! Number five!"*

"Fine!" I exclaim. "Fine. Just . . . just give me a minute, okay?"

"Just throw off your robe and get in here!"

I close my eyes, take a deep breath, and strip.

"Yes!" Liss yells. *"Dive in!"*

And I do.

And it's *freezing.*

I come up for air. *"Holy shit, you guys!* It's like swimming in the Arctic!"

"Well, it is November," Liss reminds me.

"But it's supposed to be a heated pool."

"And it's almost three in the morning," Evelyn says. "They're not going to heat it now."

"Right."

"Come on! Let's play Marco Polo!" Liss yells, and closes her eyes. "I'll go first! Marco!"

Evelyn and I rush away from her, and I get caught first. We swim and play like that for what feels like hours. We do somersaults and backflips and handstands in the water (good practice for #2). Evelyn and Liss take turns doing cannonballs and jackknives, and after a while, I forget that I'm naked or even that they're naked. It's just so much fun being here in the middle of the night with my two closest friends (or rather, my only two friends), swimming a good five hundred feet in the air with all of the city below.

And then we hear a rustling at the door.

"Oh fuck!" Evelyn yells. We race toward the edge of the pool. I jump out and throw on my robe right before the door opens and a security guard walks in.

I look over at Evelyn, who's dressed and laughing, and Liss, who's naked and fumbling with her robe.

"Hey!" the guard yells. He's old, maybe nearing eighty. "What are you girls doing up here?"

"Hi, Officer!" Evelyn sputters through her laughter.

"He's not a cop," Liss mutters.

Close enough, I think. Son of a bitch. Now we're in trouble.

"We were just swimming, is all!" Evelyn says this all flirty and giggly.

"You are not supposed to be here at this time of night, especially doing whatever it is I know you were doing." He adjusts his glasses, probably to see if he can catch a view of Liss, who's still tying up her robe. Ugh. Dirty old man.

Then he puts a finger up. "You girls wait here while I go get the police!" And miraculously, he turns right back around and heads out the door.

"Wait? What?" Evelyn laughs. "Did I just hallucinate that?"

"Um, no," Liss says.

"Where's he going?"

I'm shivering and my heart is beating a million miles a minute. "I thought you said there was no security guard at night!"

Evelyn shrugs. "Guess I was wrong."

"Let's get out of here," Liss says.

We count to sixty seconds to let Mr. Buzzkill get in the elevator, and then we sneak out the stairwell.

We have to run down twenty-eight flights of stairs, dripping wet and naked under our robes. I can feel my thighs chafing together, and I know that Liss and Evelyn don't have this problem. They're giggling in unison, but I'm utterly pissed.

But then Liss turns back to me and whispers, "When we get back, you can cross off number five!"

And my mind turns to this day—this whole entire, perfectly wonderful day. To the yoga and the dancing and swimming naked in the middle of the night.

I scurry down the stairwell behind them, smiling all the way.

9

The hallway's buzzing. Everyone's on a post-Thanksgiving, pre–winter break high. There's only three weeks of classes left, which makes everyone freak out, about their grades or their college applications or their ACT scores. The only thing I'm freaking out about right now is seeing Daniel again and figuring out the rain check situation.

But I haven't seen him all day. I run to Marquez's class, taking the steps two by two. I'm out of breath when I get to the door. I peek inside, but Daniel's not there yet, so I slide into my desk and try to calm myself down.

Play it cool, Georgia.

Everyone is deep in conversation around me. I play with my phone and pretend to be busy. The bell rings. I look up at the door. No Daniel.

"Okay, people!" Marquez yells. "Let's get started!"

Damn it. Where is he?

No one listens to Marquez, so he tries again. "The bell

has rung," he yells. "Everyone take a seat!" No one pays attention to him. He's lost all control. They all go right on talking.

And then Daniel runs in. He's about to head to his seat, but instead he looks straight at me and comes my way. My heart is in my throat. It's as though I'm still running up those steps.

"Are you going to Avery's party?"

"Yes!" I say. "I'll be there!" I feel like I'm yelling. I feel like I'm not playing it cool at all.

But he's so nice. "Good!" he says. And then he puts his hand on my shoulder and squeezes it tight. "I want to hang out!"

I'm melting. His hand feels so good. I'm about to say that I want to hang out, too, when Marquez starts flipping the lights on and off like we're in the third grade. *"People!"* he yells. *"Have a seat already!"*

"Oops!" Daniel laughs. He lets go of my shoulder and runs to his desk. Everyone quiets down.

"If we do not begin at precisely two twenty-seven P.M.," Marquez intones, "the administration is going to come in here and strip me of my tenure!" He's not really mad at us—he just likes being the center of attention and ruining my chances of connecting with hot guys.

"Now, you had an actual standards-driven assignment due today." He drops his voice to a whisper. "But please, don't tell anyone about this. It'll destroy my reputation."

Ah, that old Marquez. He's a laugh a minute.

I shuffle through my backpack to dig out my paper. We were assigned a one-page proposal previewing our chosen artist and our motivation for choosing him or her for our midyear project. Today, we're meeting with Marquez individually to get approval. I've titled my project "Parallel Uplifts: An Exploration of Lee Mullican, California Painter." I printed out copies of a few of his paintings, in case Marquez isn't familiar. I don't expect that he is. My mom always talked about how he was one of the most underrated painters of the twentieth century. She thought it was a crime that no one, except for the art historians on the West Coast, had heard of him.

"You will all work on your sketches or paintings—or whatever you want, really, your math homework, your dating schedule, your nails—while I meet with you individually."

Marquez calls people up one by one. He starts with Eddie Yang. Because our names both start with A, Daniel and I are going to be last up. Marquez's sole purpose in life is to do things opposite of their normal order, even the alphabet.

My sketchbook is pretty full, so I spend half the class drawing in whatever empty spaces I can find and half the time working on my chemistry homework, which is like trying to learn Mandarin. I've never been so close to failing a class before, but chemistry seems to be my Achilles' heel. Oxidation numbers and covalent bonds and complex ions. And crazy Zittel yelling at us if we walk behind his desk ("Do not invade my van der Waals space!"). When will I ever have to use this shit in my life?

I bet Daniel is good at chemistry. He'll have to use it. I glance over at him. He's busily painting at his desk (he creates these sorts of geometric mountain landscapes, and he's pretty good at them). I should just go over there and ask him for help.

And I'm about to, but Marquez yells out, "Mr. Antell, come on up! You're the next contestant on *The Price Is Right!*"

That's weird. I should be next. Working from the bottom up, Askeridis should be before Antell. I wonder why Marquez skipped me.

Daniel sets down his paintbrush, picks up his paper, and heads to the front of the classroom. I overhear them talking about Paul Cézanne, Daniel's chosen artist. I should have guessed from his stuff that he would choose a post-impressionist. Makes sense.

They're chatting and laughing and getting all chummy-chummy. I look at the clock. Only three minutes left until the bell. I guess I won't have time to meet with Marquez today. Sucks. I was actually looking forward to hearing his opinion.

Daniel gets the thumbs-up from Marquez and goes back to his seat.

The bell rings. Marquez turns his head toward me, winks, and points his index finger, like he's looking down the barrel of a gun. "I have not forgotten about you, Miss

Askeridis. I'd like you to stay for a few minutes, if you can."

My heart drops. Shit. Am I in trouble? I've been trying not to miss his class. Why does he want to talk to me?

Everyone packs up around me and disperses out the door. I take my stuff over by Marquez's desk and sit down. As Daniel passes by me, he presses my shoulder *again* (siiigh) and whispers, "Good luck!"

"Thanks," I say. Dear Lord, I think I need it. I'm about to get busted for all the cutting.

Then Daniel adds, "Don't forget about Saturday!"

Yes! Zero to eighty in 8.2 seconds. How is it humanly possible to be simultaneously terrified of the imminent consequences about to be imparted by an angry teacher and elated to the point of dizziness?

"I'm tying a ribbon around my finger so as not to forget," I muster like a total dork. A ribbon? Around my finger? Liss is right. I am eighty.

"Great," he says as he follows the last few students filing out the door.

Holy hell. I'm a wreck. I'm shaking with dread and excitement and nervousness.

I place my paper on Marquez's desk, but he doesn't sit down. Instead, he picks up his keys and says, "I'd like to walk with you for a few minutes, if we can, Georgia."

"Um, okay."

"I want to talk to you in private, but we're not allowed to meet with students alone in our classrooms—lawsuits and such, you know."

"Oh, right."

"I thought we could go out to a bench and talk about your art."

My art? What art? My feeble attempts at creative expression? And he *doesn't* want to talk about my delinquency?

"Sure." I shrug. It's like forty degrees out, but what do I know? I pick up my paper, zip up my coat, and put on my hood.

He locks up, and we head outside.

It's only been a few minutes since the last bell of the day, but already the campus has emptied out. The winter cold makes people disappear.

We sit on a bench right outside the front door.

"Show me what you got." Up close, I can see that Marquez is older than I ever realized before. He smells old, too—not a bad old, just like aftershave and oranges. He kind of smells like my dad.

I hand him my paper. "Lee Mullican," I say.

"Yeah? Of the Dynaton movement?" Whoa, he knows exactly who he is. My mom would have loved Mr. Marquez. "Well, that's obscure. Why, may I ask?"

"Well . . ." I fumble, "he was one of the most important artists of the twentieth century, and yet one of the most undervalued."

"How exactly did you hear about him?"

"Oh, my mom was a huge fan," I say. "She wrote her graduate thesis on him."

"Ah . . ."

"Yeah, and I always liked his stuff okay, but I never really understood why she loved him so much. So I'd like to use this assignment to figure it out."

"I see." Marquez is half skimming my paper, half listening to me. Then he puts down the paper and turns to me. "Look. I said I wanted to talk to you about your art. Here it is: You're good. Very good."

Say what now?

"Out of the one hundred and fifty students that pass in and out of my classroom each year, I see about a dozen or so truly talented ones. But usually, I only see one or two each year who have the gift. This year, I see it in you."

"What gift, exactly?"

"You are an artist. Sure, you have a lot of work ahead of you, but you have what I can't teach: vision and clarity and depth. You say something with your work."

"I do?"

"And better yet, you don't even know it." He shakes his head. "I love it."

Well, this came out of left field. A) Marquez is not being sarcastic and snarky for once, and B) he's telling me I'm good at something. Like, for real.

"Thank you, Mr. Marquez," I say. I'm stumped for more words. I wish my mom were alive so I could tell her. I'm finally doing what she wanted.

"I'm worried, though, that you might lose yourself in this project. It sounds like Lee Mullican was your mother's muse. I don't want you to get consumed by her artist."

Wait, what?

"You can focus on his art, if you want." He shrugs. "Just be careful not to lose sight of yours."

Ouch. That's kind of harsh. As though I can't have my own voice and do this, too? I mean, I was never planning on losing myself in anything.

But all in all, I still have to say, cordial Marquez is much more pleasant than caustic Marquez.

"Also, stop skipping class. You're too much of a good kid to be a loser."

Ah, there it is.

"Now, go home, warm up, and keep sketching. I expect to see great things."

He stands up, shakes my hand, and walks back inside.

I sit there a while in the cold, thinking about what he said.

I'm well on my way to crossing off #6. Learn how to draw, like Mom.

I don't care if he thinks I might "lose sight" of my art.

I know this, for sure: She would have been so happy.

10

Avery Trenholm's party is the exact opposite of what I thought it would be. Liss said it was invite only, but I thought that was just a guise for it being open to everyone except dorks, nerdherds, emos, and wannabes, and that the party would be a swollen mass of drunken seniors guzzling kegs upside down and writhing to some lame-ass house music or some such scene. As it turns out, it actually was invite only, and there are only about fifteen people here, who are all just huddled quietly in the candlelit living room, sipping on something they're calling Jungle Juice. I think it's a mix of Kool-Aid and vodka with frozen fruit in it. How very classy.

Everything about her house is catalog perfect. Gray walls. Sleek gray leather couches. Odd table-side sculptures of human forms. Over the gray marble fireplace, artsy black-and-white photos of unnamed skyscrapers are juxtaposed next to equally artsy black-and-white photos of Avery when she was a kid, five years old maybe, and then in middle school, and then last year the whole family, her wide, smiling face sandwiched between her mother and father, all three faces monopolizing the frame.

She's got the fireplace lit, snow is falling outside, and this dim winter's evening, everyone I've known since the first grade suddenly looks so adult. Maybe it's just that I haven't really spoken to any of them since we were twelve. I swear it was only yesterday that we were all wearing pigtails and swapping friendship bracelets. I don't know where time went.

I also don't know how Liss convinced Avery to include Evelyn and me on this Very Exclusive List even though I couldn't be included on the cheer squad; but we're here, and I think I might be having some sort of out-of-body experience.

First of all, Avery Trenholm is being nice to me. When I first walked in, she gave me a hug. It was the World's Most Awkward Hug, but still she reached her arms out and wrapped them around my neck for a good half second. She smelled like a mix of vanilla and Jungle Juice, so I could probably just credit her sudden familiarity to the fact that she was inebriated and didn't know who I was. And now she's laughing and smiling at me like I'm actually part of the group. Chloe, too. Then again, I think I've been too hard on Chloe. She was never really that mean to me. And actually, a few of the cheer girls are here and they've all acknowledged my existence in one form or another (while all year I've been another body in the hallway). I keep sort of looking over my shoulder because I think they must be looking at someone behind me, but they're not.

And I'm drinking, too, which is a first for me. Of course, I've consumed plenty of Evelyn's special brownies, which always lead to a weird combination of elation and hallucination, but beyond the random sips of wine and ouzo (blech) my dad has given me ("She should know what it tastes like"), I've never been drunk, and I've never had more than maybe an ounce of any kind of alcohol. It's different, this sensation of drinking—I'm just calm, and my bones feel heavy, like they're filled with water. And I'm only on my second glass of their Kool-Aid creation.

There's also the additional fact that Daniel's here. And he's sitting on the leather couch right next to me. We're so close, our arms are touching. I can feel his skin against mine, his muscles, his every little shift and laugh. Everyone's talking and laughing around us, but I hardly hear any of it. I'm in this long tunnel where everything is dark and relaxed and happy and all I see at the end of it is Daniel Antell.

I look up at him.

"Hey," I say.

"Hey." He smiles.

"How are you?" I ask.

"Pretty good," he says. "Pretty good. Glad to be here, I guess."

But then that's it. He doesn't ask how I am or say anything else to me. Five days ago, he was all excited about "hanging out" with me at this party, and now here we are, and he's not saying more than ten words.

Don't think, Georgia. Just drink.

I take a sip of juice and look over at Liss. She's sitting next to Gregg and she looks pretty happy, too—her face is all red and shiny. She told me on the way here that she's been practicing her tribal moves for later. Tonight's the night. Actually, in like an hour, I guess. She's planning on sneaking out after the socializing calms down so they can go back to his place and do *it*. Crazy. She's really going to have sex with Gregg. She's going to take this giant leap into adulthood and sexuality and all this stuff that requires responsibility and maturity and—holy shit—condoms. She's going to have to use real-life unwrapped Trojan condoms out of a box tonight. That's insane.

Don't think, Georgia. Just drink.

Jungle Juice, good. Responsibility, bad.

My glass is getting empty again rather quickly. Chloe leans over and fills it back up. I should probably slow down.

I listen to the talk about getting carded at the 7-Eleven and spring break in the Bahamas and safety schools. I have nothing to contribute, so I take another couple of sips of juice.

And then they all start getting nostalgic, as though senior year is coming to an end tomorrow. They talk about parties and dances and football games and soccer games and it's like they're speaking a foreign language—it's like I've been living in a completely different world. I look over at Liss and Evelyn, who are listening and laughing as though they were there, too, living these normal high school lives with these people, when we all know for a fact that none of us have.

But then they start reminiscing about teachers and classes, and I tune back in. Avery and Chloe are telling us about Mr. Fillmore, our sophomore-year history teacher who mysteriously disappeared after wearing bunny slippers to work and muttering about UFOs and the Second Coming; and about Mrs. Stanfield, everyone's favorite English teacher, who was diagnosed with cancer last year. They're talking to Liss and Evelyn and me as though we didn't know. I've sat next to these people for nearly twelve years. We know the stories. We know the same people. We've been there the whole time. What strikes me as I take another sip is that I don't think *they* realized it.

"And Linberg's fucking crazy," Avery remarks. "Like she might be absolutely certifiable. She's been around forever, makes no sense, old as hell, and still, she's back every August, her hair dyed a darker shade of brown."

I chime in, hearing my voice aloud for the first time all night. "And she doesn't look at you when she looks at you. Instead, she stares at the space above your head—"

Daniel laughs and adds, "*Yes!* And it's fucking creepy!"

"I think she's looking at our third eye," Liss says, suddenly the expert on all things metaphysical.

"Kind of, man," Evelyn says. "It's more like she's looking at your aura, except she's not seeing it." I get why Liss and Evelyn get along.

Avery adds, "We were always cheating in that class. I'd look over Rosie Cabrillo's shoulder to get the answer, and then I'd turn around and tell Althea White, who'd turn around and tell Felicia Carter, who'd spread it to the whole class."

Everyone except me, I think.

Don't think, Georgia. Just drink.

"And then," Avery continues, "Linberg would inevitably yell at poor Rosie, even though she was the only one who understood trigonometry. Seriously, she was the only one actually doing the work."

I remember that. How Rosie Cabrillo, freakishly smart nerd extraordinaire, would sit in the front row with Avery and some other moocher next to her, and she'd have her nose headfirst into her trigonometry book. She taught herself all of it from start to finish. Rosie's so smart—way smarter than I'll ever be. I never understood why she gave all the answers away to people like Avery Trenholm. Maybe it was the only way she knew to survive.

"Oh!" Liss adds. "And she'd stare above our heads at the corner of the room." Liss had Linberg last year for AP calculus.

"Yes!" Avery is nearly yelling now. "Oh my God, this one time freshman year, Kevin Lee did the craziest thing—"

"I remember this!" I say. I know what she's talking about, the crazy stunt that Kevin Lee pulled that almost got *me* killed. I remember it well. I sat in the back row, right next to the scene.

"You do?" Avery looks at me like she's never seen me before.

"Yeah," I say. "I was in class with you. I sat right next to Kevin, in the back."

"Oh. Yeah. You were, I guess, huh?" Nope. She doesn't remember at all.

But Avery still smiles. And it's so freaking weird because it looks genuine. Or drunk. I'm not sure. "So, tell everyone what happened!"

"What?"

"You were there. Tell the people the story!"

Everyone's looking at me, waiting to hear how Kevin Lee almost ended my life.

Daniel nudges me. "Tell us!"

Okay.

I take a sip.

"So this one day, Linberg has to go to the bathroom or something, and she leaves us all in the room by ourselves. Well, needless to say, this is a very bad idea.

"Kevin Lee decides he's going to climb up on a desk to draw some faces in the corner of the room, I guess to give Linberg something to look at while she stares over our heads talking about vectors and shit.

"So first, he stands up on the desk, but he can't reach. Then, he piles up one desk upside down on top of the other and starts balancing on the wire basket that, you know, sits under the seat of the chair."

Everyone's murmuring and laughing and shaking their heads.

"He's drawing this face in the corner of the room, balancing and drawing. Now, mind you, the window is wide open. Third floor, man. Top of the building.

"So of course, he's drawing and drawing—a little stick figure with hair and glasses, if I remember correctly. And then he slips—*slips!*—and the desk flies—"

Evelyn screams. "What happened?!"

"He almost fell out the window!"

"*What?* No way!" Evelyn and Gregg and Liss and Daniel and Chloe and everyone are all laughing and drinking.

I continue. "There I am, his black Converse teetering on the edge of the metal base of the desk. He tumbled down, his ponytail swinging, his arms flailing, toward me. I ducked because I thought he was going to land on me. And he almost did, except that somehow, at the very last moment, I moved—my body and desk together as one entity—away from his trajectory. Maybe I'd learned something of value in that class, after all. Anyway, he landed flat on the ground, right on his back. It's a wonder he didn't die."

"Oh, and the *best* part," Avery screams, her drink sloshing around in her glass, nearly splashing out. "Where did the desk go?"

Everyone except for Evelyn and me chimes in: "Out the window!"

Avery cheers: "*Yes!* A fucking desk flew out the fucking third-story window—and no one noticed!"

And there it is. Avery and I are best buds, drinking and laughing and telling grand old stories about our old high school days together. This Jungle Juice is awesome stuff.

"Wait—so how did Linberg not notice this?" Daniel asks. "I never heard this part of the story."

I finish the story. "So Linberg comes back, and Kevin's flat on the ground, and a desk is missing, and we're all laughing and screaming—and so, what does Linberg do? She turns on her overhead projector, picks up her pen, and continues her lecture about SOACAHTOA. That's it. She doesn't ask, doesn't notice. Just goes back to inverse functions or whatever shit she's trying to teach us."

"You're hilarious, Georgia," Avery says to me. "The way you tell a story. I never knew how funny you are."

"Yeah, well . . ." I don't even know what to say.

"So, Georgia . . ." Avery leans in. "Tell us about the list—your bucket list or whatever. What's on it?"

"Wait, what?" I freeze. "How do you know about that?"

"Evelyn and Liss told us about it before you got here. It sounds really awesome."

I look at Liss and then Evelyn. "You guys told her?"

"They told all of us!" Avery says. "Tell us more, though. They wouldn't tell us what's on it."

Liss takes a sheepish sip from her drink.

I want to kill them both. They told Avery and Chloe and all these other strangers about my list. They told *Daniel* about my list.

"I always wanted to make a bucket list," Chloe says. "Like stay up all night and kiss in front of a sunrise. It's so romantic."

"Is that on there, Georgia?" Avery says. "Who do you want to kiss?"

And she laughs when she says this. It's a cold laugh, and right after, she gives Daniel a pointed look. We're not best buds anymore. It's like we're twelve again, and she's teasing me. I can feel it.

"I don't want to talk about it," I say. "It's personal."

Daniel bumps his elbow into my arm. "You don't have to. I just think it's cool that you're doing something like that."

"Whatever." Avery shrugs. "I was just curious, is all."

And then, that's it. End of story. End of my short-lived glory as life of the party. They turn the focus to their upcoming trip to Belize. Daniel and Liss are leaving in one week. Daniel fills the awkward space between Liss and me with facts about Belize. The horrid humidity. The lush, tropical rain forests. The amazing barrier reefs. Their efforts in marine conservation.

I wish I were the one going instead of Liss.

Snorkeling. The Mayans. Limestone caves. Daniel.

And then something changes.

Liss and Daniel smile at each other.

It's a weird smile. A knowing smile. An intimate smile.

What the fuck?

Am I so drunk I'm imagining things?

First she tells everyone about my list, and now she's flirting with Daniel?

No. Gregg sees it, too.

He frowns and pulls Liss's chin toward him.

They kiss.

Chloe pours more juice into my glass.

I take a sip.

And another sip.

And I drink until it's empty.

"So, Avery," I say. "I have a question for you. Why did you pick what's-her-face, Zebra-girl, no, what'd you call her, Liss?"

"Georgia . . ." Liss shakes her head at me. "Stop."

But I don't stop. It was funny, what she said, and I have to remember it.

"No, wait—" I laugh. "Hold on. Oreo cupcake. Yeah, that's it. You said she looked like an Oreo cookie cupcake."

"Georgia, really. Stop it."

"No, wait. You're right. She had a name. Mary. Yeah, Chloe's cousin Mary."

Avery looks at me confused, but all nice and curious, like she's really, deeply invested in what I'm about to say. "What about her?"

"Why'd you pick her instead of me for cheer? I mean, she's a freshman and she's just as fat as me. And I could do a cartwheel, but she can't. So, what the fuck? Why didn't I make the team or squad or whatever?"

"Damn it, Georgia," Liss nearly hisses at me. "Shut up already."

"What? You said it," I say. "I'm just pointing out the blatant nepotism that runs rampant in the halls of WHS."

"Georgia," Liss sort of quiet-yells. "I. SAID. SHUT. UP."

Avery just laughs kind of fake to blow it off, but everyone else gets real silent, real fast.

Evelyn breaks in, just to fill the air with something. "So, um, Daniel, when do you guys leave for your trip?"

"Oh." He doesn't want to answer. "That first Saturday of winter break. We'll be gone the entire time."

And then they all sort of join in, all except for Liss, who's obviously pissed, but she's so far away, and I can't feel my fingers, I can't feel my tongue, I can't feel anything, really, everything around me feels so heavy and slow.

So, I lie back.

And then,

I'm there with them, in Belize.

I'm snorkeling next to Daniel.

His hand is in mine.

The waves ripple around us.

Colorful, tropical fish tickle my skin.

"Hey, Georgia, want to try it?"

Someone's handing me a net to catch a fish.

I could learn how to fish here.

That's item #8, I think.

"Georgia . . . hello? You want to try it?"

It's Evelyn's voice, calling to me from beyond a barrier reef. What is she doing here in Belize?

"Georgia—"

"What?"

I open my eyes.

I look up.

Oh, dear Lord.

I fell asleep on Daniel Antell.

Holy Mother of all things good.

What have I done?

I lift my head off of him. I wipe the corner of my mouth.

I drooled on Daniel Antell.

I look around, and everybody's staring at me. I sit up. Daniel's wiping off his arm. "Are you okay?" he asks.

Damn it all. And Evelyn, who's sitting on the floor beside me, is poking me and asking me something.

I wipe my chin. "What did you say?"

"Wakey, wakey, Georgie-girl. It's happy fun time." Evelyn's holding a Ziploc bag with crumpled leaves of pot in one hand and a glass pipe in the other. She's oblivious of how mad I am at her. "Time to spark some bud."

I wipe my eyes and look over at Liss.

How long have I been asleep?

It sort of floods back—what Avery said to me, what I said to Avery—along with a raging headache.

"Come on, Georgia," Evelyn says. "Let's give it a go, shall we?"

"Oh, my head," I blurt out. "It's pounding."

"Perfect." Evelyn laughs. "This is medicinal. It'll make your headache disappear!"

"Wait, what?" I look at Avery. "We're smoking that here? Inside? What about your parents?"

"They don't give a shit." Avery laughs. "They still smoke down here at night when they think I'm asleep or when I'm cheering away games. They won't even notice the smell."

I'm still groggy and drunk, and the room is spinning like I'm at the center of a tornado. "I don't know. That doesn't sound like a good idea at all. And anyway, I'm not so good at inhaling."

And then Avery to Liss: "I thought you said she was cool."

There it is.

It's out in the open, in front of Daniel and Chloe and everyone. Georgia Askeridis is a loser. She writes dumb lists, says mean things, rats out her best friend, falls asleep on people, drools on them, and can't inhale to save her life. After a sudden ascent up the social hierarchy—an acceptance, if you will, into the home of Avery Trenholm—comes my quick descent into dorkdom. Who knew it would all end so quickly?

"May I speak to you in the other room, please, Georgia?" Oh, great. And as a result, I've pissed off Liss. Shit.

I get up off the couch and follow her into the kitchen.

I don't want to fight with Liss. So she told them about my list. Who cares? This is all dumb. "I'm so sorry. I've never drunk this much, and apparently I can't because it makes me say stupid shit. I'm really sorry, so sorry." My head is pounding so bad. "And I fucking fell asleep. I just guess I couldn't handle all that juice—"

"What? Oh, I don't care about that. Look, Evelyn's the one who started talking about your list. I tried to stop her—I mean, I did stop her from telling them more. And as for Avery, she's idiotic. And she's so drunk, she won't even remember any of this by Monday."

"Oh." Okay. Well, then. Phew. "What, then?"

"Gregg, that's what. He's an asshole who's being an asshole."

Besides her inability to curse creatively when she's drunk, what she's saying doesn't add up. Nice Gregg? Sweet Gregg? Perfect Gregg? Well, that doesn't make sense. "What's going on?"

"He fucking called me cheap and easy."

"Wait, what? He called you that? I don't believe it. . . ."

"Well, believe it. He said I'm throwing myself at Daniel, of all things. I mean, Daniel. Why would I even do that? Gregg took me in the other room and told me tonight's not happening. He said I'm too drunk and he's pissed about me going to Belize, that he doesn't trust me."

"Holy shit." I rub my eyes. How long *was* I asleep? "I don't understand. I thought things were going well. Are you *sure*? I mean, you've been drinking a lot." *And I saw it, too. I saw how you looked at him.* "I mean, we've all been drinking a lot. Are you sure that's what he meant?"

"God! Why are you defending him?"

"I'm not defending him. I just think it was a misunderstanding, is all."

"Fuck it all, anyway." She slams her palm on the granite counter and then spins around and opens the fridge. "I need a beer." She grabs a bottle, twists off the cap, and chugs. "Screw it. This tastes like piss. I'm getting high."

This could be bad. "Well, wait a minute. Slow down. Is that really the answer?" Ugh. I sound like my dad.

"Yes, it's the answer. God. Avery's right. You *can* be so fucking uncool sometimes, you know that? You sound like your dad."

"Don't get mad at me. What the hell did I do?"

"Nothing. Nothing." She retreats and shakes her head.

"Well, why am I here, then, if I'm so uncool?"

"Forget it."

"No, why, Liss? Why are we in Avery's house? Why are we kissing up to these jerks?"

"They're Gregg's friends, that's all."

"Okay, so fine. You're kissing up to make nice with Gregg. Whatever. But then I don't understand: Why are you mad at *me*?"

"You could be on *my* side, you know."

"But I am on your side—"

I think.

She's not listening, though. She's drunk on anger and beer and juice and Lord knows what else. She chugs the bottle and throws it empty into the sink. "Where's Evelyn? Let's get this party started already."

And then she's gone.

And I'm here in No-Woman's-Land—no, strike that—No-Liss-Land, alone.

★   ★   ★

Evelyn lights up and passes around the joint, and at first I
pass, but then I see Liss sitting next to Daniel, and she's
laughing and flirting, and they're still talking about fucking Belize.

And then she places her hand on his biceps,
and he smiles,
and he leans in close to Liss
to Liss, of all people,
my best friend,
my only friend,
and the next time the pipe comes around, I think, Fuck it,
and I try,
I really try, but I cough so much Avery laughs, and then
    even Chloe laughs,
Chloe, who I thought was kind of nice—
and Liss doesn't bother to defend me this time.
But I try it again, anyway.
I breathe it in,
and I hold it,
and I breathe again.

And then.

I'm kissing Gregg.

I don't know how this happened.
His face is on mine, and mine is on his, and he tastes
    like earth and sweat and salt.

His neck is smooth.

His cheeks are smooth.

His lips are smooth.

We're on a bed.

Inside a guest bedroom or Avery's room or Avery's parents'?

I don't know.

We're on a bed, and it's dark, and he tastes like earth and
    sweat and salt.

And it's my first kiss,

and my second and my third,

and then, I lose count.

And I want to stop,

but I can't.

He tastes like soil.

I think I know this to be true.

And then,

Liss opens the door.

And then,

She turns on the light.

And then,

I'm running.

Liss screams behind me.

And then, I'm outside,

And the snow burns my bare feet.

I can't find the concrete,

If only I could find the concrete,

I know it could be warmer.
I crawl on my hands and knees and dig for the concrete.
I know it will be warmer.
I think I know this to be true.

And then,
Liss screams at me,
but I can't hear her.

And then,
my mother is there, standing
in front of me.

She's a Picasso.
Her breasts hang heavy.
Her thighs thick and round.
She's a leaf,
a pendant,
a chandelier.

She's a Mondrian,
all black and red,
rectangle and line.
She's a blue square.
A back alley tag.

She's a Mullican,
radiating spheres of needles
her face brown with dried blood.

And I am inside,
pierced with the promise of the sun.

She is right there,
her hand on my cheek.
It's warm and it's real.
I know this to be true.

I don't know how I made it back home last night, but I'm
in my bed and I don't want to get out. I don't want to
open my eyes, I don't want to move my body, but my
body has to pee, and I need coffee and water and something in my stomach, something to help this feeling of
death under my skin.

I roll myself out of the covers and force myself to look
in the mirror.

What have I done?

Oh, Mom, what have I done?

This wasn't on the list.

I eat lunch alone, and I walk home alone, and I spend
nights alone. I write to her, and I call her, and I text her,
and I try to stop her in the hallway, but it's no use. Liss
won't let me say what I want to say.

Evelyn texts that she's sorry—first about telling everyone about the list (she didn't know it was a secret) and then
about the pot. It was laced with something, she thinks,
and she's sorry. She says she wants to hang out, but she's
the last person on earth I want to spend time with.

I'm over it. All of it. The drugs and the drinking and the just fucking up in general.

I skip Marquez's class all week just to avoid seeing Daniel. No need to share any more crazy with him. I consider it my last, well-deserved sin.

As for Gregg, thankfully I don't see him all week, but the Friday before winter break he walks up to my locker just as I'm packing the last of my stuff before heading home for the two weeks.

The halls are mostly empty except for a few stragglers who are exchanging presents and cleaning out their lockers. No one got me a present, but then again, no one's really talking to me, either.

Gregg hovers over my shoulder. "Happy holidays," he says all smug and smarmy, a Santa hat hanging over his brow.

Ugh. What a creep.

I ignore him. I focus instead on my locker. There's not much in it, a few books and some extra clothes, but I'm stuffing it all in my bag, just to keep busy, just to avoid looking Gregg in the eye.

Daniel walks up to his locker. Fuuuuuck. Worst timing.

"Hey, bro," Gregg says to Daniel. Ugh. He would use a word like "bro."

But Daniel ignores him. He just opens his locker and starts packing up his stuff, too. Oh, how I wish I could tell him how it was just all a terrible, awful consequence of a series of terrible, awful mistakes and stupid, stupid hallucinogens. How I wish I could start all over again.

And then, out of the corner of my eye, I can see Liss down the hallway. Holy shit. Really? I've managed to avoid these people all week, and now the universe conspires against me to put me in the most awkward position ever?

And Gregg is standing there, his back against the neighboring locker, staring at me, smirking. "I haven't seen you all week. Where you been?"

"What do you want from me?" I finally snap at Gregg.

"I enjoyed what happened that night at Avery's. . . ." He says this low, with a crooked, creepy smile on his crooked, creepy face.

"What? How—" I murmur low. "How can you say that? Liss is my best friend. . . ."

"Yes," Gregg says. "I know that. And I feel awful. Really, I do."

I can't see what Liss ever saw in him or especially why I kissed him, but I can see why she believed everything he ever said to her. He says this like he believes it. He's good at pretending to be sincere. I think he even convinces himself that what he says is the truth.

"But you're so different," he continues. "You're so . . . pure or something. Innocent. I like it. Not like Liss."

Ugh.

What a fuckhead.

That's just disgusting.

I can see that he believes this, too.

I want to hit him.

So I do.

I hit him on the face. My palm whacks his cheek—twice, actually—and he jumps back, and I jump back, and I can feel all eyes on me—Daniel's and Liss's and those of random strangers in the hallway. Crinkled Christmas paper falls from their hands.

"What the hell?" He holds his red cheek in his hand.

"Gregg, I hate to disappoint you," I say, "but you're never going to find a girl better than Liss. And you're an asshole for trying."

I slam my locker shut, turn on my heels, and head toward my best friend.

Maybe she'll see what I've done and forgive me. Maybe she'll see that I saved her from what certainly would have been the worst mistake of her life.

She gives me a look of death, shuts her locker, and runs away from me.

Daniel runs past me toward Liss. They're out the door, together.

I deserve that.

There's nothing I could say or do that will change what I did.

But I'm sorry.

God, am I sorry.

For so many things.

11

Two weeks of winter vacation. Fan-fucking-tastic. Two weeks of sitting at home, alone, watching TV, and playing on my phone. After four months of not logging on, I check Instagram, but it's really not that interesting since I don't follow that many people—mostly my suburban cousins posting happy-family pictures of them sledding and ice-skating and other Rockwellian scenes. Liss is on all the time, but I never post anything. I check to see if she's blocked me yet, but she hasn't. I guess she has better things to do, like fly to Belize with Daniel Antell. I see that on the first day of break, she posted a photo of the runway before she left Chicago O'Hare International Airport (#goodbyesnow #belizebound #wanderlust #adventure) and then the next day, she posted a shot of her legs in a hammock and palm trees in the background (#hammocklife #travel #belizecity #neverleaving). And then that Sunday, she posted one of her standing in her bikini on the edge of a boat: "Great day snorkeling the Belize Barrier Reef. Turtles, sharks and stingray. #unbelizeable #youbetterbelizeit #bucketlist." Avery and Chloe like this. Ugh.

I look out the window. No palm trees here. I wish I could say that winter in Chicago looks as pretty as a postcard, but the truth is that it doesn't. All of that snow that's been accumulating over the past few weeks started to melt last week when the temperatures rose for a few days, but then it got cold again, which means the city streets are now blanketed by huge drifts of frozen brown slush. You can't walk three feet without slipping. I went down to Walgreens on the first day of vacation to buy some wrapping paper for my dad's present (socks and undershirts—it's what he asked for), and I nearly broke my neck. It's the opposite of romantic. It's a veritable winter wretchedland.

At least on break, I can sleep all day.

At least on break, I don't have to talk to anyone.

At least on break, I don't have anyone else to piss off.

I shut off my phone and go to bed.

I spend the first few days of vacation reading and sketching and watching shitty movies on Netflix. Considering everything that's happened, it's not so bad sitting here, doing nothing. I don't know why I ever tried doing anything in the first place.

But it's Christmas Eve. I should do something. Really. My dad will be home from work soon, probably in a bad mood since Christmas is on a Thursday this year, which means he has to close the restaurant on a weekday and, of course, also means money lost.

I don't think my brain can take any more inane suggestions from Netflix. (*Based on your taste preferences: Witty Independent Romantic Dramedies Featuring a Strong Female Lead and Anime!* Huh?) And my back is starting to hurt. I peel myself off the couch. I can work up some last-minute Christmas spirit before Dad gets home. Maybe dig out the decorations. Light some candles. Muster up some goodwill and joy. Positive thoughts, Georgia. It's been a while.

I can do it, I think. My mom was always able to make the day mean something, even when things were awful. Maybe because it wasn't about her—it was about us. Last Christmas, my mom somehow got us excited about the holiday, even though she had just come home from the hospital after having her fourth stent in six years. That last one was an especially rough procedure since they had to reach a part of the heart that is usually pretty hard to get to, and she was in the CCU for ten days before she could come home just two nights before Christmas Eve. Still, through her breathing tube, she instructed us to "get everything ready for Christmas." A few Christmases before that, she wasn't feeling well, either, because she had just started dialysis, so we skipped going to Oak Lawn and stayed home and watched *A Christmas Story, It's a Wonderful Life,* and *Miracle on 34th Street* while my dad threw together a pastichio dinner. Even so, every year she directed my dad and me to get a small tree and pull out all three boxes of decorations from the communal basement, and I'd drape the entire house in twinkle lights and foil garlands. And somehow she always managed to fill the living room with mounds and mounds of presents. I think she shopped all year and hid them under her bed. It was usually cheap crap from the sales racks of Marshalls and World Market, but she loved watching us rip open our gifts and the wild mess of papers that we'd have to swim through each Christmas morning.

This year, we've only really managed to buy a tree. Well, it's not quite a tree. It's a tiny rosemary bush that my dad bought at Trader Joe's last week, but other than that, the decorations consist of a string of picture-perfect photo cards sent by the various branches of the suburban clan and other long-lost relatives and compatriots of my dad's who check in only once each year when the U.S. Postal Service allows them to conveniently relay how wonderful and perfect their lives are without actually having to talk to us. We haven't sent Christmas cards in five years, maybe. Last week, one night at the restaurant, Dad asked me what I wanted for Christmas, and I didn't have the heart to tell him that he's not supposed to ask, that Mom never asked, that asking ruins the fun. Instead, I told him some art supplies, canvases and pastels and new oil paints, and he lit up when I said that, so I guess that's good. There will be some presents.

I can salvage this. I dig through the crap drawer to find the key for the basement storage gate. I head down the back stairwell to the basement and unlock the gate. I switch on the light. Each tenant has been allocated one ten-by-ten section of space for whatever stuff won't fit into our apartments, like the bikes we never use, the suitcases we never pack, and, of course, our dusty holiday decor that we need only once a year. There are two other apartments in the building, one above us that houses a young hipster couple and one below us where our landlord lives. Janice is a crusty old woman who owns like ten different buildings in the area. We hardly talk to any of them, which is fine. It's a quiet building, fairly cheap. That's all that mattered to my parents.

Young hipster couple's space is filled with things like kayaks and tents and skis. Janice's space is filled with furniture—mattresses and dressers and chairs. She sometimes rents empty apartments to vacationers or businessmen. I think landlording must be her life because there are no other signature details here to define her. Or maybe she has other spaces in other buildings where she stores her personal stuff.

Besides the bikes and the luggage we never use, there are boxes of books and papers down here that are all my mom's. And not just a few. A dozen boxes, at least, all from her grad school days. Mostly books on postmodern art and all of her research on Lee Mullican. She couldn't bear to throw them out, I guess. Besides that last letter, she never wrote anything personal, but she saved everything she read. This is my inheritance. Old musty books in an old musty basement. They're all mine.

Fortunately, the Christmas boxes are right at the edge. I lift the flap of each one. I don't need the ornaments, so I put that one aside. The second one has stockings and Christmas books that my mom used to read to me each Christmas Eve when I was a kid, but I figure Santa isn't coming tonight, so no need for that stuff. The third one has most of what I need. I hoist it out of the space, lock up the gate, and carry it up the steps back to our apartment.

I dress the living room in garlands. I wrap the twinkly lights around the fireplace that's never worked. I plug them in and shut off the lamps. That's a start. I dig into the box and find a few candles—cinnamon spice and pine—and I light them. At least we'll have a hint of home-baked cooking and deep forest air. I pull my dad's presents out from my closet and place them next to the little rosemary bush on the coffee table. There. That's a little better. It's starting to feel like Christmas in here, after all.

My dad's key rattles at the door. I run to open it.

"Merry Christmas!" I yell. I'm smiling for the first time in two weeks.

Dad looks at the room, drops two heavy bags full of food from the restaurant on the dining room table, turns on all the lights, and goes into the kitchen without saying a word about the decorations. Without wishing me a Merry Christmas back.

"Dad?" I follow him into the kitchen. He's taken off his hat and heavy coat and thrown them on the counter. He's drinking a glass of water and shaking his head.

"What's wrong?"

"Georgia . . ." He says my American name. That's not good. "Your art teacher, what's his name? Mr. Marquez? He called today."

Oh, shit.

"He calls to tell me that you are not going to school. That you are missing for a whole week? What is going on?"

What the hell? Marquez rats me out on Christmas Eve? I thought he believed in me. I thought I was his star student.

"Dad . . ." I could tell him everything. That I'm also failing chemistry. That my heart's broken in eight million pieces. That I'm alone. That I've made terrible mistakes. That I miss everything about how it used to be. That I tried to keep my promise to her, but I failed.

No words come, though.

"Where were you?" he demands.

"Nowhere," I mutter. "Starbucks. Burger King. Just sitting at random places, reading and stuff." *And getting high,* I think.

"Why you are not in class? What does this mean?"

"No reason. Just . . . really, Dad. No reason."

His eyes scan my face. He's searching for something in me, but it's like he doesn't really see *me* standing here before him.

He walks past me into the dining room where he left the bags of food. The heavy smell of chicken and potatoes seeps from the bag. There's probably enough there for tonight and tomorrow, for our holiday dinner.

He pulls out a chair and sits down. I join him.

But there's nothing to say.

He stares at his hands. "No more of that, okay? I mean, what will people say if they hear Georgia Askeridis is running around the city, cutting school and all this?"

What people? We don't have any people.

"I want you to be a good girl. You are always good girl. *Kaló korítsi,* okay?"

"Okay." I nod.

"Mr. Marquez, he says that you have a big project coming up. A big art project? You have a lot of work, yes?"

My Mullican project. I haven't worked on it in weeks.

"You do good on it, and he says he won't record all the absences, he won't tell the principal. You have to go to him on Monday after your break ends with this big project finished."

What? It's not due for another few weeks, after break. Is Marquez seriously going to make me work on my supposed vacation?

"You can do that, yes? Then you will not get in trouble, he says."

"Yes, Dad. I can do that." I say this, but it's the last thing I want. To spend my lame vacation obsessing over a dead artist who my dead mother obsessed about.

"Good, then." He nods to himself and then looks at the bags of food. "Let's eat now." He stands up, unloads the Styrofoam containers onto the table, and then shuts off the lights.

The Christmas lights twinkle again, but it just doesn't look the same.

My dad leans over and kisses me on the forehead. We eat in silence with the TV on while the candles burn down to nothing.

When I was fifteen, I chipped my front tooth while eating an apple. The dentist, Dr. Crespo, said that I was most likely grinding my teeth at night, and he prescribed a $350 night guard that was supposed to relax my muscles and clear up the terrible headaches I'd been having for over a year. His assistant put some plastic goop in my mouth, had me bite down, and created a mold that was used to shape the night guard, which I was supposed to wear every night. When I went in a week later to try it on, Dr. Crespo had me put the guard inside my mouth and sit for a few minutes. Drool poured out the corners of my mouth. "Your brain thinks that there's food there, right?" he said. It felt more like someone's knuckles were digging into my jawbone. "But after a little while, a few minutes, even, that sensation will fade away. Your brain will stop registering the awkwardness and your body will ease into the discomfort." I drooled for another couple of minutes and then it stopped. He was right. I hardly even felt it in my mouth.

I spent two months trying to wear the damn thing. Every night, like clockwork, I put the plasticized sentinel into my mouth and fell asleep. And every morning, like clockwork, I woke up to find the damn thing on my pillow or lost in the covers or sometimes even on the other side of the room—on the floor by the door or somewhere on my desk. I'd chucked it in the middle of the night. Even while unconscious, my body didn't want to experience the sensation of someone digging a fist into my face.

Go figure.

Life without Mom is a little like that. At first, it was all pain and tears. Every day was hard. I'd wake up, and the sun was there, still shining in the sky, but the world didn't make sense anymore. Then, little by little, especially with the list, that pain faded even more. I cried only once a week instead of every day. And then I even stopped crying. I moved forward.

Christmas feels like someone stuffed that night guard back into my mouth and stitched my lips closed. On the outside, I'm keeping it together for my dad, but inside—inside—there are no words to describe how deep the hole goes.

We do it, though—Dad feigns surprise with his undershirts and socks, and I actually am happy to receive the art supplies, though now they're a bit tainted with the errors of my ways.

At the end of the day, after the presents and the leftover chicken and eight hours of Christmas reruns on TBS, I pack up the garlands and lights and candles, and Dad puts the box by the door so I can bring it back downstairs tomorrow. We survived. Another holiday without Mom.

I take the box down to the basement and dig out a few of Mom's boxes to carry back upstairs. It takes a few trips, and I'm out of breath after the first actual exertion of energy that I've had since the tribal dance class. I throw the boxes on the floor of my room and collapse beside them. I went online and found plenty of basic info on Lee Mullican, but I have this feeling that I need to find something else. I don't care what Marquez said. This isn't about losing myself. It's about finding her. It's about understanding her. There are just so many questions I didn't get to ask: Why didn't you follow your own advice? Why didn't you do everything? Why weren't you the one who lived a life without fear?

I feel like her obsession with this Mullican guy might give me some answers. And if I'm going to paint something meaningful, I have to understand why this guy mattered so much to my mom. This is as much about me—and my unanswered questions—as it is about her.

First I read her thesis. It's seventy-three pages and titled "Unifying Forms: Male and Female Energy Bodies in Lee Mullican's Work." It's long, well written, and overly academic. I learn about Eastern meditation practices (which my mom never did), receive more verification that she adored his work to no end, and am ultimately convinced by my mom that despite the fact that he was a male artist working in a male world, Lee Mullican was a feminist at his core.

But it's not what I want to find. I dig through the boxes. They're filled with photocopied papers from the LACMA and Smithsonian libraries, copies of other people's essays, and old photos and Lee Mullican's sketches. I was too young to understand what she was doing, but I remember these same papers piled on the dining room table. We ate in the living room for a few years until she completed her final thesis and show, and then, except for the paintings, she finally moved everything downstairs.

I keep digging until I find my mom's copy of *An Abundant Harvest of Sun,* the book that accompanied the LACMA exhibit. I remember when she bought it. I remember when it was brand-new. Now it's worn and tattered and musty from being in the basement for so long.

I also remember her obsessively poring over this book. This was before you could find a lot of stuff on the Internet about him, and she liked it because it had good reproductions of his most famous paintings. I flip through the pages, through the accompanying pictures of his paintings and sculptures. Mullican loved the abstract just as much as my mom, but his paintings were more ethereal than hers. They look like cave paintings or crop circles or postmodern stained glass for a church where the attendants are all stoned.

I skim his bio. Lee Mullican was a bit of a hippie. At one point, he said that he sought "the opening of a new world, opening the mind into a kind of cosmic thought," and then it continued into her most favorite line: "ideas that went beyond what one saw, beyond form." My mom underlined this two times and gave it a big heart. I believed her when she said that she had never done any hard drugs, but I really can't believe she never, at the very least, smoked up. I mean, she was an art major. I guess I'll never know. I page through the book. I'm amazed to see so much of his hand in my mom's hand. He loved pattern and repetition and color, and so did she. Because of him, she used a printer's ink knife when painting so that the color popped up out of the canvas, the rhythmic lines created a three-dimensional effect. Mom did this with her women's bodies that now line the walls of our hallway. She liked to make them blur and zigzag. Her women were tribal. They danced.

Except for that last letter to me, she never wrote down anything personal, but she loved to write in all of her books—underlines, stars, reminders to herself in quick scribbles. This one is filled with her notes. I run my finger across her handwriting. Mine is exactly like hers. It's like I could have written them.

I wish I could talk to her about why she loved this guy so much. I like his work fine, but she loved it. Was somewhat consumed by it. She had other painters she loved, too—the big names of the post-impressionist and modernist periods, as well as lesser-known surrealists such as Yves Tanguy and Man Ray, but she felt a kinship with this man in particular. She said once, "It's as though he's painting my soul." I was too young to ask why. And now it's too late.

Instead, this is what I have:

She has highlighted: "As you are working through this process of painting, the painting's there . . . but you've gone through this metaphysical process . . . more than anything. And it's a meditative act . . . the canvas is there before me. And it's this attitude that makes the painting appear . . . and you're not quite sure how it got there."

And beside it, she wrote: "YES. Extension of self/yet not self."

And this: "I pulled the essence of nature down over my head." Next to it, her handwriting reads: "Submersion/ retreat. How to live fully engaged and still maintain separateness from suffering, from failure?"

She has underlined and starred: "The freedom of abstraction appealed to Mullican, the fact that an abstract painting could 'be upside down, it can be any way, and it's still okay.'" And next to it, she's written, "Like life."

She wanted more for me even though she couldn't do more for herself. Even though she felt like she was submersed in her own failures. She wanted me to be the brave one. She wanted me to do everything.

But being brave isn't about living every minute exhilarated. It's about waking up and knowing that despite the worry and the sadness and the deep, dark fear, you're going to go forth anyway. That you're going to try anyway. That you have a choice, and you're going to choose to live, today, bravely.

Maybe that's all any of us can do. Maybe that's all I can do.

My mom did that, for a long time. She lived bravely through the hospitals and the procedures and the constant fear of death. The reality of the inevitable.

Maybe she didn't realize it, but I know she tried. I know she moved through each day with the suffering and the fear, as well as the desire for a fully engaged life, as best as she could. She was the one who kept us going.

And she's gone now.

But it's okay.

It's still okay.

Life will turn us upside down, and it will still be okay.

My mom thought so. Lee Mullican thought so. Sitting here on my bedroom floor, surrounded by nothing else but the ghost of my mom's infatuation with another ghost, I don't have much choice but to think so, too.

I'm trying, Mom. I'm really, really trying.

Dad bought me some cold press illustration boards and a new set of gouache paints, which was what I had asked for. Considering I missed a good fifteen hours of Marquez's class this semester, I have a lot of catching up to do. Five paintings and a seven-page reflection paper. And now I have to finish it all in a week.

It moves slowly, this act of creation. I try to make it meditative, like Lee Mullican described. I try to just make the canvas appear, but I'm rusty. I put oil on the canvas, but there's nothing there. I have nothing to say. I don't know how to make the metaphysical real.

Maybe I should call up Evelyn and enjoy one more round with the brownies. That would get the juices flowing. That would get this project done.

Ugh. I know that's a very bad idea, for multiple reasons.

Reason #1: Ever since the party, I've been blowing Evelyn off. She's texted at least six times that she wants to get together, but I've been lying and telling her I'm sick. Which is kind of true. Technically speaking, I'm

afflicted with something bad, like a severely allergic re-
action to drugs and other human beings.

Reason #2: Evelyn's sweet and all, but I can only take
so much of her. She's so far on the edge of not caring
about anything—school, college, family, state and federal
laws—that she wears me out. Without Liss around to bal-
ance her out, I don't know how much of her I can take.

And then there's Reason #3: I made a promise to myself not to get high anymore.

Shit. Now, why'd I go and do that?

I check my phone. Evelyn hasn't texted since the day
before Christmas Eve.

This was our last conversation:

Her: *hey what's up?*

Me: *Nothing. Sick. You?* (I refuse to misspell my texts.)

Her: *nm. get 2gether?*

Me: *Sorry. Can't. Achoo.*

Her: *ok. feel bettr. merry xmas.*

Me: *You too.*

And that was it. I haven't seen her in two weeks. Anyway, it would be just a bit awkward to text her out of the
blue and say, *I want brownies. I want to get high.*

So I sketch and I paint and sketch and paint, but after
a full day's work, I have nothing—a few ideas and one
messed-up canvas—hopefully I can paint over it tomorrow. And hopefully I can fill up the other four with something respectable.

I pull out the list. #6. Learn how to draw, like Mom.

I need to do this. It's as much for me as it is for her.

I made a promise.

I pack up all of Mom's Lee Mullican papers and carry them to the basement, and then I head back to my room. I have no other place to work. Mom had a studio she worked out of, but we closed it up when she died.

I shove my bed out from the center of the room against the wall. I push aside my desk, pile up my dirty clothes that cover the floor, and stuff them into my closet.

I put on my favorites: Lorde and Jack White and First Aid Kit, and yes, even some Taylor Swift, and, of course, Nina Simone. I blast the music, and I force it out.

I force myself to do this.

First, I draw faces on my paper. My face. Her face. His face.

I glance at photos, but mostly I work from memory.

I copy them onto a canvas. I sketch the lines of our faces, mix the colors with my knife. Cadmium red and yellow ochre with a dab of titanium white turns into my mother's hair, which is also my hair. Ivory black mixed with burnt sienna and a bit of the yellow becomes my father's hair.

Terra rose and cobalt blue for our skin.

Viridian for our eyes.

I etch lines like Mullican's crop circles onto our cheeks. Our eyes fade into our skin. Our jaws fade into the ether. We form a triptych. A blurred map of a lost land.

I refuse the real. I embrace the abstract.

I eat bowls of cereal and toast with peanut butter and cold bacon-and-egg sandwiches brought home by my dad, who ignores my locked door.

I sleep in two-hour spurts and then I wake up and paint again.

I am outer world and inner world.

I am energy.

I am vision.

I am Lee Mullican.

I am Diana Melas.

I am Georgia Askeridis.

On the sixth day, I go to bed at eight A.M. after a full night of painting my last canvas, and I sleep for sixteen hours straight. I wake up to the sounds of firecrackers and horns.

Oh right, New Year's Eve. I squint in the dark at the clock. Midnight. I guess I missed the countdown. Maybe Dad knocked on my door, maybe not. It doesn't matter. All I know is that the worst year of my life is over. Hallelujah.

I turn on the light, but the rods and cones in my eyeballs protest. I'm groggy and starving and surrounded by a mess. Even though I put down old towels, I dripped paint all over the carpet. I should have used a tarp. Dad's probably going to kill me when he sees this.

Nothing I can do about that now.

I feel like I spent the last six days dreaming, but when I look, the paintings are really there. I don't know if they're good. I don't care, really. I see them, and they're mine. They're the first real productive thing I've done in months. Or maybe ever.

I reach to my nightstand and check my phone for the first time in a week.

Three messages, all from Evelyn.

Her, four days ago: *u better?*

Her, two days ago: *hello? call me. im worried about u.*

Her, yesterday: *did u see insta? u ok, georgia? call me if you need to talk.*

Instagram? Why the hell would I be on Instagram? Like I could give a shit.

I don't want to go on Instagram. I don't want to know what other people are doing. And I certainly don't want to think about the fact that, come Monday, only a few short days away, I have to actually face Liss and Daniel and Evelyn and Gregg and Marquez in the living flesh. I don't want to go back to reality.

But I can't help it. Her fucking text has piqued my curiosity. Now I need to know.

I open Instagram and scroll down.

There it is, three photos down. I know exactly why Evelyn texted me.

There's a beach, a sunset, bare feet. *Skinnydipping! Second time in three weeks. #life #love #friends.*

And she's tagged four people: *Daniel Antell, Felicia Carter Kevin Lee, Rosie Cabrillo.*

She did #5—again, and without me—and even worse, with Daniel. And that probably means she also did #15, with Daniel. I bet she kissed him. I bet they're together now. I mean, she tagged him first in the damn post.

It's really not okay.

So much for new beginnings.

So much for positive thoughts.

I reach into my bag and pull out the list.

Do Everything? Be Brave?

Fuck it all.

I rip up the list into a dozen tiny pieces, and then I throw it in the trash.

I turn off all the lights and dig my head under the pillow. I scream into the mattress in a lame attempt to drown out the blasts of celebration that reverberate through the city.

Sorry, Mom. I failed you.

This is also what it was like:

> She had curled up on the couch,
> three blankets over her near-naked body,
> the TV blaring, with Ellen or Dr. Oz or Alex Trebek.
> It didn't matter. It was noise on the screen,
> and she wasn't listening.
> She had destroyed them all.

> She worked for months on them,
> her canvases. She'd sketched and planned
> and worked and worked, but then,
> it wasn't right. None of it.

So she blacked them out and came home.
I'm done, she said. *There's nothing left.*
And: *They'll forget me when I'm gone.*
And: *I'm almost gone.*

She was fever and chills, sweat and tremor.
I could blame it on what we didn't know:
the sepsis in her veins, the infection as insidious as fear.

But it only made her speak what was true.
I'm the broken one, she said. *Everyone knows it.*
I'm their mirror, a reminder of their own deep sorrows,
how far down they're buried in their old, hurt souls.
There's nothing left for my art to prove.

I begged my father.
There's nothing I can do, he said.
I was the one who called her doctor,
told him she was sick again,
that she wasn't making sense.
But it was different this time.

The urge to destroy is also a creative urge.
It was different this time
because she knew exactly what was coming.
She knew it was the last time,
for her.

part two

12

I trudge through the snow with my art case by my side. I'm weighed down on all sides, textbooks pulling me backward, squeezed by the many layers of winter clothes—two sweaters, a down coat, scarf, hat, and gloves, all black. (I've given up on fashion.) Two inches of snow and a windchill of twenty-five. In April. First day of spring was two weeks ago. Oh, Chicago, you sadistic city. When I was a kid, my dad only read the d'Aulaires myths to me at bedtime. I think it was the only way he could think of to try to make me Greek. My favorite was about Hades, lord of the underworld, who captured Persephone while her mother, Demeter, cried above. I liked the idea of the pomegranate seeds, how the cold, hard winters were caused by Demeter's angst during Persephone's time in hell. The freezing wind slaps my face. It seems as though Demeter is especially pissed this year.

I push myself forward into what is nearly a blizzard. Of

all the places my dad could have chosen to move to, he chose Chicago? He had sun and water and mountains and olive trees, and he chose this? A city full of congestion and potholes and snow that turns to giant piles of slush? I know he left for a better life. My mom liked to remind me of that—of the sacrifices he made so that I wouldn't live in poverty like he did. But so many Greeks went to Australia and Florida. Not my dad. He had to come where winter rules most of the year.

I walk up to this building, Webster High School, which is my Own Personal Hell. It's like I'm Persephone; I'm the one stuck here with no way out. Today is going to be like every other, where I spend my days ducking in and out of classes, talking to no one, my hood tied tight around my jaw. Evelyn transferred to Choices mid-January after she was caught selling pot. We text occasionally, but we never actually speak. I miss her, but she's also part of a time in my life that I wish I could forget.

Liss and Daniel returned from their trip tanned, blissed out on Belize, and chummier than ever. They won't make eye contact with me, yet I could hardly get through the entire month of January without hearing about their trip: from strangers in the hallway ("Oh my God, the rain forest! Could you imagine?"), from our crappy little school newspaper ("Central America Biology Expedition: Exclusive Interview of Environmental Heroics!" Hyperbole much?), and even from Marquez ("So, Mr. Antell, did you stay out of trouble? No smuggling illicit substances in prehistoric vases, I hope."). Liss and Daniel are always together, and usually, Avery and Chloe and their respective boyfriends are not far behind.

The other thing is that Avery and Chloe are on this new mission to, and I quote, "be nice to everyone. To end the madness of high school gossip." That was in the paper, too. I guess Liss has bought into this PR stunt. She's with them all the time. And despite the fact that they'll smile and wave at me, I refuse to believe it. And Liss refuses to talk to me.

I'm alone, but that's nothing new. It was like that before Liss entered my life. I should have known it would be like that again.

It's also been months since I turned in my project Monday morning, 8:03 A.M. on the dot, per Marquez's instructions that were relayed from my dad to me. But he never said anything about what I did, just put a checkmark in the book and handed it back to me a week later. He probably just figures he was wrong about me. He's probably sorry he ever sat me down on a bench in forty-degree weather.

It's fine.

My sole purpose in life is now this: Get Through Senior Year. One more month. That's it. Walk through the door, go to class #1 (Twentieth-Century World History), sit down, do my work, leave, rinse, repeat (times twenty-nine more days).

The only thing I have—the only thing I like—is my art. I draw every day, and I occasionally paint on the weekends.

It's not for the grade.

It's not part of the overarching Get Through Senior Year project.

I actually enjoy my time alone in my room, immersed in my own projects, learning new techniques off You-Tube. It's the only time I enjoy being alone.

I was wait-listed by the University of Illinois Urbana–Champaign, but I'm getting comfortable with the thought of staying at home, working at the restaurant, and going to city college. I've been spending a lot of time with my dad. Well, at least in the same room as my dad. We don't talk much. Not that there's much to say. I spend afternoons at the front of the restaurant, studying my chem homework (I think I can, I think I can), sketching, and working the register while my dad preps and cleans and cooks. I know he likes having me there, and I know he can use the help.

In return, he gives me enough money to pay for my classes at the Soul Power Yoga studio, of all places. Ironically, it's the one thing from the list I've kept with. I've become somewhat addicted to the place, going to tribal yoga and the other basic yoga classes. It's about the only time, other than when I'm painting, that my brain is not replaying that night with Gregg. It's about the only time I can breathe.

I push open the door. The outside air suffocates me with its chill, but the air inside these hallways is worse. I've stopped using my locker since the location smack-dab between Daniel and Liss is the worst kind of asphyxiation imaginable. I head straight to history. I take a seat in the front row, pull out my notebook, and start copying the agenda from the board.

I'm a good girl now.

Just like my father wanted.

Daniel's standing at Zittel's door when I get there for second-period chemistry. He's leaning against the door frame with his arms crossed and hair mussed, looking all GQ-ish, and I'm so mad at myself for fucking it up with him. Liss deserves him. And I mean that in the best possible way. They're both good people, and beautiful, too. They make a pretty couple.

I just about bolt. I could hide in the bathroom for a few minutes, tell Zittel I'm having lady issues to shut him up about me being tardy—but then Daniel looks me in the eye and smiles, his signature smile, warm and kind.

"Georgia! Finally. I found you. Here." He hands me a folded sheet of paper. "I can never catch you in Marquez's class. You always disappear right when the bell rings. Meet me at Ellie's after school, okay? We need to talk."

I open my mouth to say something, but I'm choking on the toxic air of Zittel's ammonia solution seeping out from the classroom, mixed with a healthy dose of absolute shock.

"See you later," he says.

And then he bolts.

I stumble to my desk and open the paper.

Three words:

She misses you.

What is he doing? Meet him at Ellie's? Is it just going to be him? Or will Liss be there, too? Why is he getting involved?

I haven't learned much from Zittel, but I do know this: Never mix certain chemicals, like ammonia with bleach, because the subsequent vapors could knock you dead.

I miss Liss, too, but I don't know if it's worth it—the two of us in the same room at the same time. And with Daniel in the mix as well.

We might very well need emergency assistance.

I avoid making eye contact with Daniel, but I can feel him staring at me over Marquez's balding head. Now that it's nearing the end of the year, Marquez has pretty much stopped teaching and he lets us do whatever we want, as long as we're there and turn in a set amount of pieces every two weeks, and as long as we keep sketching.

I try to focus on my Sharpies—black and gold and red—on this rhythmic, patterned piece that requires my very careful attention. It's too hard, though. My hand is shaking. I have too many questions in my head. Fifty-two minutes until Ellie's.

I put aside my project and pull out my chem book. Zittel told us today that if we get a C on the rest of our tests, we can get a C in the class. The next big one is two days away. I guess a bunch of us are failing. Big surprise, considering the man can't teach to save his life. Here's hoping he curves the scores.

I open to the homework. This is what it says:

Practice Questions: Write the balanced equations for the following reactions.

1. $Na + H_2O \rightarrow NaOH + H_2$
2. $C_2H_6 + O_2 \rightarrow CO_2 + H_2O$
3. *Ammonium nitrate decomposes to yield dinitrogen monoxide and water.*
4. *Ammonia reacts with oxygen gas to form nitrogen monoxide and water.*
5. *How many grams of ammonia, NH_3, can be made from 250 grams of $N_2(g)$?*

And on, and on, and on.

It's a fucking foreign language.

But hell, it gets my mind off Daniel for a bit. I'm moving letters and carrying numbers and determining some kind of solution, even though I have no idea if the solutions are correct. Zittel said we had to at least try, so that's what I'm doing.

I look up at the clock. Five minutes left.

I can't help glancing at Daniel, who feels my gaze. He looks up from his project, gives me an enthusiastic thumbs-up, and mouths, "Ellie's!"

Hollow. Pit. In. Stomach. Growing.

"Miss Askeridis," Marquez yells across the room. "May I speak with you after class?"

Ugh. Now what.

I look back over at Daniel, who is shaking his head. "Not today," he mouths.

"Sorry, sir," I respond. "Can't today. Have an appointment."

But Marquez caught Daniel's silent directive, so he responds accordingly, "Ah. A hot date with Mr. Antell?" *Oh. God. No. Don't be a smart-ass now, Marquez.* "Well, that can wait." He glances at Daniel and then back at me. "This can't."

I look at Daniel and shrug, and he shakes his head.

"Wait for me?" I mouth back to him.

He nods in response.

Everyone around me is laughing and whispering and oohing and aahing like they're nine years old.

Fuuuuuck.

One more month.

Twenty-nine more days.

Just Get Through It, Georgia.

You're almost out of here.

Everyone packs up and leaves, and like last time, Marquez leads me out the door toward a bench, except this time it's even colder than it was in December. I wrap my scarf around my mouth, but it doesn't really help. My nostrils are freezing. My cheeks are freezing. My eyeballs are freezing.

Marquez is just wearing a sweater, though.

"Aren't you afraid you're going to get pneumonia or something?" I ask.

"Cold like this is good for the blood," he says, shaking his head. "Keeps us alive."

Okay, crazy guy.

We sit there, watching the students scuttle away. Marquez stares off into space, not saying anything.

My butt is starting to freeze now, too, and all I can think is that I wish I had a longer coat. That, and I wish I were at Ellie's. Or then again, maybe not. I don't know anymore. Ugh. What does Marquez want?

"So . . . you wanted to talk to me?"

Marquez turns to me. "You're right. I did." He smiles. "I never had children."

. . .

"I sometimes wish I did."

. . .

"I'm not going to say that if I could have had a child, she would have been like you, because that's a strange thing to say—"

. . .

"But I will say this: She would have painted like you. She would have drawn like you. She would have had your hands."

Oh.

"My sister owns this little coffee shop, over on the West Side, near the Ukrainian Village. She also hosts little gallery shows every month. I showed her your work."

Oh.

"It's kind of short notice, but she'd like to include you in a show coming up in May. You'd be showing with a couple of other artists. College students whose work is at a professional level. I think you should start thinking of yourself as a professional, too. You're still raw, as you should be, but you're good. But that means you'll have to create more pieces. They want a bunch to pick from, and then they choose that night which ones to show."

I'm absolutely, utterly speechless.

I've got nothing.

No words. No vowels. No consonants.

Nothing.

I'm a dissolved liquid.

I'm vapor.

"There's one problem," Marquez says. "The show opening is the same night as prom, so you wouldn't be able to go."

"Oh . . ." The words come out. "Like I could give a shit about that."

And Marquez busts out in a hysterical fit of coughs and laughter. "And she definitely would have had the same sass as you."

He shakes my hand and releases me into the afternoon.

I've got to get to Ellie's.

Hopefully, I'm not too late.

I run down the street as fast as I can over the slippery slush piles. A little bell rings when I open the door to announce my entrance into an empty sandwich shop. Daniel's not here. Whatever he had to say to me wasn't important enough for him to wait ten minutes.

Damn.

"Are you the girl they call Georgia?" a voice calls from behind the register. A nerdy little guy, only slightly younger than me, gives me a big old grin.

"Yeah, that's me."

"You have been summoned here to meet with a certain Daniel A.?"

"Indeed I have," I say, playing along.

"Well, he had to dash, unfortunately. But he directed me to deliver this to you." Nerdy Guy reaches in his apron pocket and pulls out a note. Another little folded paper. I take it from his hand. "Mission accomplished. I can now go back to inspecting the fryer basket. Ah, the demands of the lowly employed."

"I can relate," I offer, and then I say, "Thanks for this."

"Anytime, my princess!"

I head outside and open the note:

Sorry. Couldn't stay. Emergency. Rain check?

That's it. No e-mail. No phone number. No inkling of a hint.

Another rain check. We all know how the last one worked out.

Like it matters.

He's with Liss now.

He's got her, and apparently, all of a sudden, I've got my art.

I'll take what I can get.

★ ★ ★

I can't wait to tell Dad about the show. I take the warm, rattling train down to the restaurant. I stare out the window and imagine sitting across from him in the booth, telling him my news, his smile wide on his face. I bet he'll say something in Greek, something I won't understand, but I won't need to understand it to know that he's proud. I'll be his *kaló korítsi,* his good girl, again.

But when I get there, Dad is in the middle of a meeting with some guy in a suit.

They're huddled in a booth, very official-looking papers spread out before them. I slide into a booth two down from them. I take out my sketchbook but am distracted by trying to figure out what the meeting is about.

It basically goes something like this: The Suit punches numbers into a very expensive laptop, then writes a number on a Post-it note and says something to my dad. My dad then peers over his reading glasses at the number. He shakes his head. It doesn't look good. They repeat this process a few more times, until finally my dad and the Suit stand up and shake hands. The meeting is over.

Dad sees me and waves.

He walks the Suit to the door and they shake hands one more time.

He comes over and sits down. "Georgia. I am glad you are here. We need to talk." He takes a deep breath and then says this: "I have to close the restaurant."

Close the restaurant? What is he talking about?

"That was Craig McIntire, our accountant. The news is not good. We finally are not making any profit at all. It's been a very long time coming, but now I know for sure."

"Wait. What? Can't we change up the place like Mom wanted?" I don't understand. He's just giving up so easily. "New booths? Coat of paint? Menu?"

He shakes his head. "No money for that."

"What about a loan? Like small business or whatever? We could save it. I'll be done with school in a few months. I could help." I can't just let him give up this place that's been more of a home to me than our home. I swallow back tears, but I'm invigorated by Marquez's faith in me. I could help redecorate the place. Make it superhip. Maybe make it an artists' mecca. We could have coffee and scones and live music and shows, maybe like the one I'll be showing at in a few weeks.

"I already took out a loan a few years ago. Can't do it again. Nothing to show for it."

Oh.

"Well, what, then? What will you do?"

"Remember your uncle Vassilis in California? You met him. He wants me to come there. He has a catering business in a city called Azusa, and he wants to expand. He needs my help."

"California?"

He nods.

He's leaving Chicago for California? After thirty years in this city, he's deciding to leave *now*?

"I want you to come, of course. You could go to college out there. They have many good schools. You could even get a job with Vassilis to help pay your way."

I blink back tears, trying hard not to cry in front of my dad, trying hard to imagine this alternate future, one that is far away from the Midwest, far from the skyscrapers and tornado warnings and winter-tainted springs. Quite honestly, I don't know what I want. I mean, this is what I want, right? I'm sick of being here, but then again, I never thought I'd actually leave.

"The sun is shining there now," Dad says. "It is seventy-three degrees today."

"And smoggy," I say. "I hear they can't even go outside some days because of the pollution."

He responds in Greek: *"H zoe einai san ena agouri. O enas to troei kai throsizete, kai o allos to troei kai zorizete."*

"Dad. I have no idea what you're saying."

"This is what I'm saying: Life is like a cucumber. One man eats it, and he is refreshed, while another man eats it, and he struggles."

I guess this is what I get for complaining about snowfall in April. My entire life reduced to a cucumber seed and then subsequently uprooted and replanted five thousand miles away.

I don't know what other choice I have. The world closes in on me. Static fills my ears.

But finally, after a few empty moments, this is what I say: "I'll think about it."

"Okay, then."

We sit in silence, both of us staring out the window at the pedestrians huddled in their layers, slipping and sliding across the icy sidewalk.

He looks at me. "Now, you tell me some news."

This is the perfect moment to tell him about my day, about Marquez and the gallery show and my future as a professional artist.

But I don't.

"I have homework." I shrug. I can't sit here anymore thinking about things that are out of my control, thinking about how everything is just so fucking far out of my control. "Big chemistry test in two days."

"Well then, you have work to do." He stands up. He is about to turn around to go back to the register when he stops himself. He takes my chin in his hand and says this: "*Eisai to ithio yia to mamasou. Oraio.*"

I understand this perfectly.

You are the same as your mother.

Beautiful.

When I get home, I google Azusa, California. I imagine sand and surf and palm trees swaying in the gentle breeze, with movie stars jogging by.

Turns out that Azusa is a long, long way from the beach, and despite its romantic-sounding name, there's not much there. First of all, the name itself is stupid. They're not sure, but it might mean one of two things: everything from A to Z in the USA (ugh), or even worse, it might stem from an old Indian word meaning "skunk place." It's known for its brewery. It had a drive-in theater that closed in 2001. An "A" is etched into the nearby mountain. And . . . that's it. Awesome.

I log off and check my phone, hoping maybe Daniel somehow got my number from Liss and texted me or something.

Nothing.

I have one thing left. My art.

I pull out my paints and dig in, working until 1:30 A.M., when I collapse on the bed.

I dream of protons and electrons and palm trees and cucumbers.

I dream in vivid color of new maps, new topographies.

I'm surfing on ice.

13

Daniel's desk is empty. It has been for over a week. He's been absent in all his classes. Word on the street is his father's sick, like really sick. I overheard a few kids in art class talking about him. Apparently, he lives here with his mom, but neither of his parents has a lot of money, and with his dad's chronic illness, it might mean they won't be able to afford college. He's been working double shifts at Baskin-Robbins to try to save as much as he can. But now he had to fly out to Oregon because his dad is having some kind of heart procedure. And I have no way of contacting him. I have no way of telling him that I've been there, that I know what he's going through.

At the end of class, Marquez hands me a stack of postcards—announcements for the gallery show. They're so official looking. On one side is this gorgeous piece that looks like an abstract cross section of human musculature. And on the other side is this:

Shikaakwa Art Gallery and Coffee House presents
Important Things
Works from Georgia Askeridis, Elsa Baines, Roberta Fernando,
and Elizabeth Revell revolve around the
themes of creation, mutation, and destruction

Contemporary art in all media
Opening Reception: Friday, May 20, 8:00–11:00 P.M.

*Whether you succeed or not is irrelevant, there is
no such thing.
Making your unknown known is the important thing.*
—Georgia O'Keeffe

There it is, my name, first in the list, with many thanks
to the creator of alphabetical order.

Okay, enough glass-half-empty bullshit.

This is really happening.

I feel like calling someone, but the only person who
comes to mind is my mom. Well, and Liss, of course.

I could give her a card, invite her. And tell her to bring
Daniel, too.

Except that prom is that night.

Either way, I want her to know that I did it.

I completed #6.

She should know.

I think of Daniel's note. I pull out a Sharpie and write
in the corner of one of the postcards: "#6. Check."

I head to my locker for the first time in months. Liss is

at her locker, talking to Avery. I open mine and pretend to shuffle my things around. I wait for them to finish up. After they leave, I run over and slide the card into the slots in her locker.

There.

A peace offering.

It's the most important thing I could do right now.

Dad is *very* excited about the show. Like, I'm kicking myself for not telling him about it last week. I haven't seen him this happy in a year, maybe.

"I will close the restaurant that night," he announces.

"Dad, you can't close the restaurant. I mean, you've never closed the restaurant."

"Eh, why not? We're going to close for good in a few months. What's another night?" He places his hand on my cheek. "Anyway, *koúkla mou,* there is no other place I would rather be."

He plants a kiss on the top of my head. "You are *my* important thing."

The next day, in the middle of chem lab, I get a text from Liss: *Congratulations.*

Huh. So, she's talking to me.

I tell Zittel I need to go to the bathroom, and when I get there, I duck into a stall and text back: *Thanks. You okay?*

A minute later, I get: *Yes. Thanks. Hope ur good.*

Okay.

I go for it: *Is everything okay with Daniel's dad? I heard the news. I hope he gets better. And I only wish the best for you guys.*

There. I said it.

It's a start, I guess. An exchange of words. The first in four months.

Then nothing, for like six minutes.

I'm sitting on the cold porcelain sink in this cold, dank bathroom waiting for the response that could bring me back my best and only friend. Ninety-nine percent chance Zittel's going to ask if "everything came out okay." I don't care. I'll stay here until the end of the period if it means a 1 percent chance of reconciling with Liss.

Then: *Not sure yet. It doesn't look good. Thanks though. Congratulations again. Bye.*

And that's it.

When I open the door to the chem lab, Zittel looks at me and asks, in front of everyone, "Did you fall in?"

Well, I took the risk and tried my chances, and regardless of the actual statistical outcome, I most definitely lost.

I spend every day after school working on my stuff. I have to bring it all to school three days before the show so that Marquez can drive it over to the gallery, where his sister is going to work on putting it up.

I've stopped sleeping, both because I'm hungry to create more pieces and because I'm a nervous wreck. I'm just too excited for the show.

Everyone else at school is too excited for prom. All I

hear all week is "prom this" and "prom that" and "Oh, my dress is so freaking awesome" and "Oh, I still gotta rent my tux" and on and on and on. All I can think is, I still have three more pieces to finish. I like mine better.

On the big day, half the senior class is absent, particularly the girls. Liss is among the absent ones. I imagine her at some beauty salon getting all dolled up, her normally wild hair being shellacked and coiffed with gel and spray. I imagine her in sequins and high heels. I imagine her next to Daniel in a black tux, their arms intertwined, posing for the school photographer, her hip jutting out, her chin slightly tilted. Ugh. It's just such a pretty image, the two of them together.

I walk into the mostly empty art room (just me and three other losers), and Marquez smiles at me. "Big night tonight!" I'm surprised he doesn't comment on the fact that on the one day I'm allowed to cut class, I actually show up. But I can see that he's not in a sarcastic mood today. He's genuinely excited for me.

I nod and head to my desk. I really have nothing to do. I'm too nervous to do anything. I have one more test left in chemistry next week (I got a C+ on my last exam! Woot woot!), and with ten days left before the end of the year, Marquez has abandoned any hint of a lesson plan for a few weeks. I think about leaving. Maybe going home and taking a nap.

Then, Daniel walks in. It's his first day back in weeks. I haven't heard any news about his dad, but from the dark circles under his eyes, I can see that he's been through hell.

He sees me and smiles. He heads in my direction, pulls up an empty chair, and sits down next to me. "I was hoping you'd be here."

The familiar hollowness at the core of my being immediately returns.

"First of all, congratulations on your big show tonight."

"Thanks. But is your dad okay?"

"Oh, well." He stops. "Yes. And no. He had an issue with his heart and needed a valve repair."

"Oh, I'm sorry. My mom had heart problems, too. . . ."

"Yeah? It's rough, right? I mean, he's just really tired all the time."

"It gets better," I say. I don't say, *And then it gets worse.* I've already said it once. I don't need to say it again.

And maybe it will be different for them.

He nods. He knows what I mean. "He's okay now, but his only hope is a kidney transplant. He's on a list." *So was my mom.* "The good thing is I think it's been a real wake-up call for him. I mean, mostly." *Not like my mom.* "I stayed for a while to help him settle in at home. I came back for the last few weeks—prom and graduation and all that—and then I'm going back for the summer."

"He'll be happy to have you there."

"Yeah, so, look . . ." Daniel shifts in his chair. "I'm sorry about that day at Ellie's. Did that guy give you my message?"

"He did."

"Good. I was waiting when I got the text from my aunt about my dad. I was on a plane that night and I didn't know your number."

"I figured as much."

"Here's the thing. I think you guys should make up. Like I wrote in that note, she misses you. She talks about you all the time. We'll be at the movies or whatever, and she'll say something like 'Georgia would love this.'"

I do that, too.

"She doesn't even hear herself sometimes." He smiles. "She's stubborn. You know that."

"Well, I messed up pretty bad. I never even wanted to do that with Gregg." I can feel my face redden.

I wanted to do that with you.

"You couldn't help it. Whatever that girl Evelyn gave us was some fucked-up shit. I'm glad she's out of this school. And honestly, I don't really get why Liss is holding this over your head so much. I get it. It was a crazy night."

You get it. You actually understand.

"Anyway, I didn't mean to wait this long to tell you, but I just wanted to let you know. And I think you should talk to her."

"I gave her the card about my show. She texted back. We had about the shortest conversation ever. And then that was it."

"You were *texting*?" He shakes his head. "That's not a conversation. Texting is about as effective as delivering the mail via pigeons. There's only so much you can communicate. You guys need to talk in person."

"Yeah, you're right." I shrug. "I'm willing to, but I don't think she is."

"Let me talk to her. I can be pretty convincing when I want to be." And he winks.

And he's so damn cute.

He's with Liss now. Let it go, Georgia.

"Okay," I say. "Well, thanks."

"Have a great show tonight." He stands up. "Mr. Marquez, I was never here."

Marquez looks at the ceiling and then under the desk. "Who said that?"

Daniel throws his bag over his shoulder.

"Hope your dad's feeling better," Marquez calls out as Daniel heads toward the door.

Daniel nods and says, "Thanks." Then he turns and waves. And he's gone.

Marquez looks at me. "You want to go, too?"

I think about it for a second and then decide to stay. I have the big show tonight, a glimmer of promise that I'll talk to my best friend, and a near-empty, quiet classroom with nothing to do but draw. For once, I'm comfortable right where I am.

The Shikaakwa Art Gallery and Coffee House is so über-cool, I can hardly stand it. It's small and the air is thick with the heavy scent of espresso and more espresso. Right when I walk in, someone dressed like a superhip penguin offers me some miniature empanadas, but my stomach is in too many knots to eat anything. If my dad's arm weren't wound around mine holding me up, I might have already collapsed on the floor, my knees are so shaky from this crazy night.

My dad accepts an empanada in his free hand and takes a bite. "Mmmm. These are very good. I should suggest something like this to Vassilis when I get there."

"Dad, I think they have empanadas in California."

"But these have kalamata olives inside." He holds it up for me to see. "It is very fancy."

The room is packed full with all these artsy people, and while I know they're all here to support Marquez's sister and the other artists (there's a lot of squealing and hugging and pointing at artwork that is not my own), I don't care. Because there they are, my seven paintings, hanging on the walls right next to theirs. I'm an artist.

My dad seems just as nervous as me, he's holding on so tight. "I called Maria. She wanted to come, but the kids are all sick. She was so very proud to hear your news."

Marquez isn't here yet, but I recognize his sister immediately. She's short like him and has the same feisty eyes. She comes running up to me and gives me a big hug. "You must be Georgia! So happy to meet you. I am Carissa." She rolls her r's like Dad. "Did you see all of your beautiful work?"

"I did," I say mid-hug. "This is amazing. Thank you so much."

"It's what I do. Give a place to new artists so they can

share their voice. It's my service to the world. Now, go, see your work—" And she scampers away to give someone else a hug.

My dad and I wander around the studio, spending time looking at all of the art. I love the other artists' work. All three of them are students at the local college, and I just can't believe I'm here with them. This is so much better than prom.

After making our rounds, we find a corner table. My dad orders a double shot of espresso and sips it slowly. "This is like being in Athena at the *kafeneion,*" he says. "Except that no one is smoking."

Marquez arrives and shakes my dad's hand, and my dad beams with pride. Carissa periodically sends a few people our way. They tell me how much they like my work. It's really crazy, all of this. Toward the end of the night, Carissa skips over to whisper that a few people actually want to buy my stuff. They want it for their homes. They want to put my art on their walls.

Unbelievable.

And then something even more unbelievable happens.

Liss and Daniel walk through the door.

And behind them, Avery and Chloe, of all people, with their arms around their dates.

They're dressed up for prom, Liss in a nonsequined lime-green eyelet dress with her hair redder and wilder and wispier than ever, and Daniel in a gray suit and vest. Avery and Chloe look a little more traditional, in black sequins and pumps, but it's the weirdest thing. They're not at prom. They're here instead.

They're here. For me.

I run to the door. Liss sees me and opens her arms.

And we hug.

It's just that easy.

"What are you doing here?" I ask. "Shouldn't you be at prom?"

"We were. It was lame," Liss says. Daniel and Avery and Chloe nod. "Terrible music. Awful food. And the ever-predictable dry humping and such. I thought Q-tip was going to have to turn on the ceiling sprinklers just to get them to separate."

God, I missed her.

"I'm so sorry, Liss," I whisper. "I fucked up so bad."

She looks at Daniel, and then Avery and Chloe, who give me a wave and then wander off into the crowd to leave us alone.

"Yeah," she says. "You did." I look at her, my closest friend. No, it's more than that—she's the only other human being on earth who understands me to the core, the one who sees me for me, the one who knows me well enough to say she's had enough of my shit. "But it wasn't entirely your fault. Gregg's the real fuckup. And Evelyn with that shit she gave you." She takes me by the shoulders, right near my neck, and says, "But don't you ever do anything like that again."

She forgives me. Hallelujah, holy shit, she forgives me.

"Cross my heart and stick a needle in my eye."

"Don't do that! You need your eyes for your artwork," Liss says. "Now, give me the grand tour. I want to see it all."

I show her the paintings: the one of my father, his face etched with the topography of the Peloponnesus, his skin lines revealing the mountains of the Demeter and Artemis; the one of my mother, her face a simple labyrinth where the beginning meets the end; and the one of Liss, her face as a map of the bus and train routes, the 22 and the 36, the Red Line and Brown Line, of everywhere we've been. There are others, too, of imagined maps, with empty faces inside. These are for sale. The first three are not.

"Georgia, these are simply . . . extraordinary—"

And then she squeezes me and whispers into my ear, "Number six was the most important one."

"You're the one who convinced me to do it," I whisper back. "Thank you."

"How many more do you have left?"

"Oh. I'm not doing it anymore."

"What? Why?"

"No reason." *Just that numbers 13 through 15 became completely irrelevant the minute I kissed Gregg and you kissed Daniel.* "Just . . . it was pointless to do it alone."

"Oh. I'm so sorry, Georgia." *Why are you apologizing?*
"Well, where is it?"

"I ripped it up . . . and threw it away."

Liss looks like she's about to smack me, but before she can say or do anything, Daniel and Avery and Chloe come back around. Of all the people to be here tonight, I did not expect the cheerleading squad to show up.

"Aren't they amazing?" Liss says.

Daniel nods. "I can totally see Lee Mullican in your work, but like, they're yours, you know?"

"You looked him up?"

"Yeah . . . I was curious," he says. "Great stuff, for sure."

Avery cuts in. "Yeah, they're, um . . ." She fumbles for her words. I don't know why, but I can't wait to hear what she thinks of them. "They're really colorful. . . ."

That's the nicest thing she could come up with?

Chloe steps in. "I think they're all so beautiful. I really love the one of Liss. I knew it was her the minute I saw it."

I have to give Chloe credit. She actually is a nice person.

"Wow," I say. "Thanks. That really means a lot."

I'm about to ask them more about prom, but then Carissa comes up to introduce me to a couple who is interested in one of my paintings. I can't not talk to them.

"Tomorrow," Liss whispers before I can get away. "Can we talk?"

I nod. "Tomorrow."

And I'm swept away to talk business with an actual art buyer.

It's all just unbelievable.

Liss and the rest of them leave for an after-party ("You should join us later!"). Around 10:45, the crowd starts to thin a bit. I wander over to my paintings, where three of them have SOLD signs attached to their corners.

Eighty dollars each. Times three. I just made $240.

I am a working artist.

But then I hear that little voice. It's my mom's voice.

This is what she's saying:

There's no money in art.

There's little appreciation.

Even Lee Mullican. He died mostly forgotten.

Even me.

They'll forget me when I'm gone.

Was it all worth it?

That was at her worst. And that wasn't even really her. That was the infection, the sugar, her slowly dying mind.

I shake that image of her out of my head and force myself to remember her at her best. This is what she would have said:

I'm proud of who you are, Georgia. I'm proud of who you've become.

This is what she did say to me.

Her letter is there in my pocket.

The night has been magical and wondrous. Yet all things magical and wondrous must come to an end sometime, so after the last few stragglers head out the door, my dad and I say our good-byes to Carissa and Marquez and head home. I could join Liss and Daniel at the after-party, but I'm just not in the mood. Or, I should say, I'm in too good of a mood. All I want right now is to be at home with Dad, to go to bed happy, and to wake up to a new morning where everything is pretty much okay.

But when we get to the car, Dad asks me if I want to get some ice cream. He's wide awake (all those tiny shots of espresso, I think), but even more than that, he's happy, too.

"Sure," I say. "But where? I can't imagine any ice-cream places open at 11:30 on a Friday."

"I know of a great little spot that serves ice cream where we will have the whole place to ourselves," Dad says.

He drives us over to the restaurant. He unlocks the door and tells me to sit in the front booth. He turns on the lights just so he can see enough to make us a sundae, then turns them all off so that the only light coming in is from the outside street lamps. As people walk by, they give us funny looks, surprised looks, envious looks.

And this is what it's like:

I'm eating ice cream in the dark front booth with my dad
with all of Chicago outside our window,
horns and taxis and sirens.
The night is alive around us.
And I can see us sitting here
just like they can see us sitting here.
I see it, and I know that this moment is good,
that this is one of the most perfect moments

of my life.
This is all I need,
right now,
to be here with him.
This is all I want.

14

It's 3:23 A.M. when I'm woken up by the annoying *ding-a-ling-ding, ding-a-ling-ding* of a text. Damn it. I forgot to turn it off. I blink my eyes and try to focus on the soft slants of light coming through the blinds. Wait a minute. It might have been Liss. That's not annoying. That's nothing short of awesome.

I jump out of bed and dig my phone out of my bag.

It's Evelyn.

Huh.

I haven't heard from her in months. She's the last person I would expect to hear from, especially at this time of night.

I hit the button to read the text.

This is what it says:

> georgia im sorry for this and for everything and u need to
> know that u were the nicest person i ever knew and thank

u for including me. tell liss too okay? my mom is making
us move again and i just cant do it anymore. i cant be stuck
like this forever. but its going to be ok i know it. it'll be fine
now that it'll be over.

I call her and throw on the lights, but she's not answer-
ing and I'm freaking out I'm freaking out I'm freaking
out.

Shit shit shit. What does this mean? What is she doing?
Why—fuck—why is she doing this?

I call her again and again, but there's no answer. I don't
know her mom's number. I don't know anything else
about her except where she lives. Where she lives. I know
where she lives. I have to call 911.

I tell the operator about the message and about the
drugs, and luckily I remember her address and her apartment number, and the operator, her voice so firm but so
human, asks me where I live and for my number and she
thanks me for calling and tells me to wake up my father.

I do, and he's confused because it's 3:30 in the morning and I tell him we have to go we have to go, but he
doesn't understand so I have to explain it all to him—what
Evelyn did—what we did, all of us together—and I'm
worried, I'm just so worried that she's done something
worse—pills or something, I don't know, it just doesn't
sound good. And he's simmering mad—his fists tighten—
his jaw tightens—he's disappointed again, the deepest
kind of disappointment I've ever seen. As he pulls on his

socks and his shoes, he mutters: "This is who your friends are?"

There's no time, there's no time, let's go already—we have to go.

We head out into the dark, chilly night. My dad drives quickly down the near-empty streets, and it's too much of a familiar feeling, this middle-of-the-night feeling, this heading out into the unknown like so many times she woke up with chest pains or she was crashing or she was already in the hospital and they'd call us to come, it doesn't look good, it doesn't look good, this might be it, this might be the last night. And then it was. But that very last night we weren't really rushing. That night we knew it was coming.

And now this again. The same unknowns. What was she thinking? What was she doing? Why didn't she choose to do something else? Anything else?

Why am I always the one they go to?

I see the flashing lights of the ambulance and fire engine from a block away. They're there already, thank God, maybe they saved her, maybe she hadn't done it yet, what-ever she was going to do, maybe it was a false alarm.

But when we pull into an empty space, when we jump out of the car, when we run to the front door, when we see the doorman's face, that same old man who caught us naked so many months ago, when we see the stretcher and the strength of four men pushing her unconscious body forward, when we see them hoist her into the back of the ambulance, we know it was too late. Again. This time. We were too late.

I don't know how they found Evelyn's mother, but she's here with us, rubbing her frail hands together, pacing up and down the waiting room floors. It took her four hours to show up, and my dad had to say something nasty. "Who are these people who leave their children alone by themselves?" I didn't respond.

But somehow she made it. Maybe she was in Omaha or Raleigh or Washington, D.C. She's rarely at home, and I've never met her. She's older than I thought she'd be. She has big brown eyes, like Evelyn, and when she looks at me, they soften.

When she first arrived, she grabbed me and hugged me. "You're her friend Georgia, right?"

I didn't know how to hug her back, how hard to squeeze.

She held on. "I don't know what I've done to make Evelyn try so hard to hurt me like she has. Did she give you any clue as to why she would do something like this?"

I didn't know how to answer. I didn't know how to say that she did, that she talked about it all the time. I didn't know how to say, *You move too much. You're gone too much. You just need to be there for her.*

And then I thought, I needed to be there for her. But I wasn't.

At that moment, I felt sick, like I wanted to collapse and let Evelyn's mom be the one to catch me.

We sat down, finally, and talked for a while about Evelyn, trying to piece together the time line between when her mom left and when she took the pills. I guess Evelyn is failing every class and her mom thought it would be a good idea to move again, this time to Nevada, where her sister lives. Her mom said that Evelyn was angry, of course. But she said that this was nothing new, and she even said, rather coldly, if you ask me, "She just brings all this upon herself."

Now we're here, the three of us, waiting in awkward silence. I can feel my dad, next to me, judging all of this, trying to piece together how I managed to surround myself with such unfavorable people, like I've been hiding my real self from him. I guess we each have secret faces that we hide from the world. Maybe Evelyn's problem is that she doesn't know how to hide them very well, that she's the most honest of anyone.

A few doctors come out to us periodically to tell us first that Evelyn is alive and that her stomach's been pumped, that she's breathing, and that she may or may not wake up today.

Also, that she was lucky. Very, very lucky. That it's a good thing I called when I did. That's what they said to me. It's a good thing.

My dad leaves at eight to open the restaurant. I don't know why he doesn't just close again today. What's another day?

Before he goes, he pulls me into the corner of the hallway.

"Your mother would have been very disappointed about this, you know. Drugs? Overdose? Friends with this kind of person? I do not want to imagine what else. I do not even know what she would say to you—"

"Dad, I—"

But he doesn't let me talk. Instead, he interrupts me with a low whisper. "I don't know who you are, Georgia. I don't know what this is about."

And with that, he turns and walks away, leaving me there, alone.

I sit with Evelyn's mom for a few hours, but there's no change, no news. Finally, she convinces me to head home when there's nothing else to say or do or hear.

I nod off on the bus, holding my bag tight to my body. When I get home, Liss is standing there, waiting for me.

She doesn't know what's happened yet. She's on the steps, staring at the clouds.

"Find any turnips?" I say.

She sees me and smiles. "Not today," she says. "A few jellyfish and snails, but no vegetables."

God, I've missed her.

I burst into tears.

She puts her arms around me. "What's going on? We're okay, you and me now, you know that, right?"

"Really? Just like that?"

"Sure . . . why not?"

I pull away from her.

Why not?

There are so many reasons for why it can't just be okay, just like that. "I don't know." We sit on the steps at the front of my building. "Here." I show her the text and I tell her everything and I'm a mess I'm a mess I'm a mess. The world is upside down again.

"We shouldn't have just dropped her like that," I say. *You shouldn't have dropped me like that.*

Liss hands me back my phone. "We hardly knew her," she says, and I'm stunned by her callousness. And then she says, "We were using her, Georgia. Both of us. We were using her to get high. I'm not saying it was right. I'm just saying that's what we were doing."

I realize Liss isn't being cold; she's being honest.

And that's why I respect her. Because she says things honestly. Even when she's angry, she speaks the truth.

I can't blame Liss for dropping Evelyn, for dropping me.

She reacted honestly to things.

Which is something I rarely do.

Because I hate feeling that way.

I hate the truth of what I'm feeling, which is absolute anger and disgust at all the things I can't control.

Sometimes you need positive thoughts, sometimes you need the truth.

And the truth is, I'm angry.

I'm angry at Evelyn for doing what she did.

I'm angry at Liss for dropping me like she did.

I'm angry at my dad for living in his bubble of grief, for ignoring me for months and then suddenly guilt-tripping me when I needed his support.

I'm angry at my mom for telling me to make that stupid list. I can't do everything. I can't be brave. And how dare she expect me to, when she couldn't even do it herself. And how dare she not take care of herself so she could tell me what *not* to do. Why I shouldn't be doing things like smoking up and kissing my best friend's boyfriend and failing at school and failing at life. She was supposed to be here to tell me *not* to do things, not to do everything.

And I'm scared, so very scared, of becoming just like her, sick and stagnant and afraid.

And then I'm angry at myself for feeling that way, for blaming her. I mean, I don't know. Could she help it? Could she have been different from who she was? Wasn't she brave in her own way? Facing all the horrible pain, in her kidneys, in her muscles, in her heart, in her life?

There was so much pain.

I don't know.

What I do know is this: I don't have to have it all figured out.

But I can speak the truth, as I see it. It's one of the bravest things I could do.

So I take a deep, deep breath.

And then this is what I say: "Look. You shouldn't have dropped me like that. I'm supposed to be your best friend. And I get it, I hurt you. I did a stupid fucking thing. But you did a stupid thing, too. You disappeared. You went to Belize and came back with new best friends—Avery and Chloe, of all people. It's like I didn't exist or something anymore to you. And now you want to be able to hug me and say we're okay and I'm just supposed to accept it?

"How are we supposed to go back to how things were? How are we supposed to pretend that I didn't kiss your boyfriend even though I didn't know what the hell I was doing? How are you going to trust me? And how am I ever going to trust you? How will I know that you won't just drop me again?"

Liss gets quiet.

Really, really quiet.

We sit for a while with Liss being quiet, thinking about what I said, not saying anything back.

Maybe she's going to blow up at me. Maybe she'll get up and walk away. Maybe this will be the end. Maybe she will drop me permanently and that will be that. Then she looks at me, her eyes red and wet. "You're right," she says finally. "You shouldn't have kissed my boyfriend, even though he's the biggest asshole in the world and even though you were fucked up and even though it wasn't really your fault. And I should have talked to you first."

"And now you're friends with Avery and Chloe? Even after what she said to me at the party?"

"What'd she say?"

"You don't remember?"

Liss shakes her head.

We were all pretty messed up that night, so I guess I shouldn't be surprised.

"She said, 'I thought you said she was cool.'"

"Chloe said that? About you?"

"No. Avery did. And last night, at the gallery: 'They're really colorful'? Like she couldn't even muster up something better than *colorful*? I thought she was on some mission to be nice to everyone. I poured my heart into those."

"She doesn't have to like them, you know."

"Yeah, but—"

"Okay, well, look: Chloe's not that bad, Georgia." Liss shrugs. "And Avery's, well . . . she's Avery. You know she wakes up at four thirty every morning just to straighten her hair?"

"That's supposed to convince me that she's a good person?"

"No, Georgia. It's supposed to convince you that she's human. That she has insecurities, just like us. And that she was high, too, that night when she said that thing about you not being cool or whatever. And she says and does stupid and mean things, just like we all do. And I mean, nobody's that bad. Don't you think we've judged them just as much as they ever judged us?"

. . .

"We're all just trying to get through, you know?"

. . .

"I mean, would it help if I said she volunteers at the hospital every Saturday? We're all just trying our best."

. . .

"Why do you care so much about what she thinks, anyway?"

. . .

"Think about Evelyn. I think she's the one who's struggling the worst. She's trying the hardest."

And she's right. About all of it.

"I *am* sorry, Georgia. Really."

"I'm more sorry. Infinitely so." The tears come now, fast and full. I can hardly catch my breath. "Like, down deep, buried into my core, is this gaping hole of remorse for what I did. I don't know that I'll ever be able to express how big it is."

Liss wipes tears from her face and smiles. "I think you just did."

"Well, okay, then." I take a deep breath. "Good."

"I have something for you." She pulls out a blue envelope with my name written on it. "Here."

I rip it open and there it is, my list, numbers 1 through 15, all rewritten in Liss's handwriting.

"I'm mostly pissed at you because you ripped it up," she says. "Maybe even more so than for kissing that fuckhead."

I don't know what to say, partly because I'm moved by the gesture, but also because I'm feeling done with it—with the idea of doing everything, of being brave, of living life for my mom when she couldn't even take care of herself enough to live it for me.

"Thank you for doing this, but, um, yeah . . . I don't think so. I think the list is over."

"What?"

"I don't really need to do everything. And honestly? I'm kind of pissed at my mom for telling me to in the first place. This should have been her list, not mine. And she should have included a point where she took better care of herself so she could be a mom and tell me how not to fuck up my life."

"Oh, come on, Georgia. You don't mean that."

"I kind of do, though. . . ."

"Really?"

"You were there. You know what happened."

"But Georgia, she loved you. She couldn't help what happened to her. She couldn't help getting sick."

"Couldn't she?"

"Why do you always do this?"

"Do what?"

"Expect the worst. Go to extremes. Give yourself over to something big, then give it all up when there's even a little bit of imperfection."

Do I do that?

"She wasn't perfect, and neither are you. And just because she died doesn't mean she didn't love you. Maybe she's not here to make you feel bad about doing stupid stuff, but I hope that doesn't mean you're going to give up doing stupid stuff. I mean, you have to *live,* Georgia. You have to fuck up sometimes. You *will* fuck up some-times. Everyone does."

And she's right. Again.

Damn it.

"Okay, fine. Let's say I do the list. Let's say I finish doing my list of stupid things because my dying mother told me to try everything at least once, even if it's throwing myself out of airplanes that are not about to crash." I point to the new, clean list written in her handwriting. "But what about numbers thirteen to fifteen?"

"What about it?" Liss says. "List or no list, you *have* to go for him. I mean, I hang out with him all the time. And he thinks you're *cute*. At least, that's the word he used."

Ex-squeeze-me?

"Wait. What? But—but—you guys. I mean, you're together, right?"

Liss bursts into this huge guffaw of a laugh. "Me and Daniel? God, no! Not my type *at all*. I mean, he's supernice, but A) he's too skinny and B) he's like a brother."

"But, wait—you guys were together in Belize, and skinny-dipping, and prom, and, I mean, you're always together—"

"'Cause we're *friends,* Georgia," she says. "That's it. Nothing else. We got to know each other when his dad got sick and my mom offered to consult with him."

Oh.

Right.

Her mom, the medical social worker and the nicest person on earth, who would do anything for anyone. And there I was, once again, assuming the worst.

"He's all yours. Really. I have absolutely, positively, no interest in Daniel Antell. Never have, never will. Besides

the fact that I would *never, ever* do that to you, I'm holding out for the college men."

Oh.

"So that changes things, then?"

Huh. "He used the word *cute*?"

Liss nods.

"That's sort of flattering, and sort of disappointing. Not
sexy? Or mysterious? He said I'm *cute*?"

Liss punches me in the arm. "You *are* cute, so just shut
up and live with it."

Well then. Daniel Antell.

"You have to do it, then. You have to ask him out.
Again."

I look at the list, at what I've done and what I haven't
done.

"I know how to do a handstand now," I say.

"Oh yeah?"

"I spend a lot of time at the studio where we took that
tribal dancing class. I'm not quite able to do it away from
the wall, but I can hold it for, like, thirty seconds."

"Rock star. You look good, by the way."

"Thanks. It's called minus ten pounds. I've been going
to Aspen's classes a lot." Not that it actually changes how
I look. By all official medical charts, I should technically
lose another fifteen pounds. But I'm not going to kill myself trying to achieve microscopic proportions. I'm still
curvy me, and I always will be.

I think for a minute. "I guess this doesn't have to be

about my mom, right? It could be about me. It could be a little bit about her and mostly about me."

"Exactly."

I look back at the list. Let's see. This is what I've completed: handstands, skinny-dipping, drawing, cheerleading, tribal dancing, cutting class, getting high, and asking Daniel out.

This is what has yet to be determined: running downhill, skydiving, trapeze school, fishing, and flambé.

Shit, that's a lot.

"Do you have a pen?"

Liss digs into her bag and hands me one.

This is what I write:

#16. *Finish the list.*

"Okay, fine. I'll do it. I'll finish the list. But I want to do some of these with you *and* Evelyn, though," I say. "Like, trapeze school—will you do that with me? When she wakes up, we'll get her to do that with us. We'll go swing like monkeys. It'll make her feel better."

Liss gives me this sorry look like she can't even pretend to promise me that Evelyn's going to wake up and that she's going to be okay and that we'll all be hanging from swings happy as can be.

But I have this fantasy: It involves getting Evelyn away from her mom, convincing her to get her GED, maybe even move with us to Champaign, where we can get an apartment and she can go to the community college down there.

"You can't save her, you know."

"I know," I say, but then I write it down, anyway.

#16. *Finish the list, after Evelyn wakes up.*

Now she has to.

After Liss leaves, I take the train down to the hospital. The only thing I've heard is that there's been no change. Evelyn's comatose. Her mom said they think she took some of her mom's Ambien and some other shit and washed it all down with half a bottle of rum.

I hate it here. I hate having to walk through these doors again. I hate having to press the buttons on the elevator again. I hate having to walk the same maze of hallways. I hate the smell of piss and blood and antiseptic and Jell-O. I hate being here, where my mother spent too much time. Where I spent too much of my childhood. I hate it.

But I have to do this, for Evelyn.

I find room 6-142. I take a deep breath and knock. Her mom opens it and silently waves for me to come in. The nurse is there, checking her vitals. She points me to a chair next to Evelyn.

It smells like hospital, and Evelyn looks like shit; her dreads have been shaved and her skin is gray. She's not intubated like my mom was, but she's in that deep sleep that I remember too well, and I don't want to be here I don't want to be here I don't want to be here.

The nurse flips her chart closed and leaves the room with no words, and before I can say anything to Evelyn's mom, like I'm sorry I can't stay I have homework to do, or I'm sorry I can't stay I have dinner to cook, or the truth, that I'm sorry I can't stay I'm going to dissolve if I have to, this is too much, I shouldn't have come, it's all too much for me, Evelyn's mom says this: "It means the world that you're here. No one else has come." And then, "Talk to her. She needs to hear us." She leaves to get coffee. She deserts me here with her in this hospital room where so many have died.

Evelyn, can you hear me?

I don't know what to say.

I have so much to say.

Mom,
You lie there,
choking on air
the blast
the force
fills you so powerfully your lungs fill and fill and fill.
There is no exhale.
Inflated, you are still conscious but you cannot breathe
    out—not on your own—
there is only oxygen.
Too much of anything can kill,
even life force.
It's like moving through the sun.
There is only gas, vapor, moving air,
light and more light.
There is nothing else.

Your heart:
I can't see it as anything but broken. I travel down a tunnel to a time when you were a child, five years old, maybe
your birthday, maybe the morning, when you first woke
up. You were open and expectant and smiling. Your mother, who I never met, was awake, maybe cooking or
maybe cleaning or maybe sitting in a chair waiting for
you, and you walked into the kitchen, where she greeted
you with everything inside her heart, her arms wide open
for your first morning embrace. You settled into this love;
it filled you. Your heart was full.

Once upon a time, your heart was wrangled from your
chest cavity, disconnected from your body, placed on a
table, and tinkered with. I remember that day. I felt you
there on the bed, feeling nothing, knowing everything.
Your heart was not your own. As the earth spun, hurtled,
carried you through space, they moved the space that was
your body, they moved you out of your body. The soul
does not live in the heart, and breaking ribs do not release the soul. It is a heart, a pump; it moves oxygen
through thin wires. The soul is in the air. The soul is in the
skin. The soul breathes and exhales every minute. That
day, the day they ripped it out of your chest, your soul was
still there, not inside you, but everywhere. I felt it.

   At the end, it was bruised.
   At the end, it was empty—the body, the heart, the mind.
   At the end, we had to let you go.

We had to.

And I'll never be sorry enough.

Evelyn,

Can you hear me?

Dad comes home with dinner—I'm guessing French dips from the smell. He sets the bag on the dining room table. I put down my book and walk over to peek in the bag. I was right. "Thanks for bringing home food," I say.

Dad doesn't look at me or say you're welcome or even ask me if I've heard anything about Evelyn. He just goes into the bathroom. It's like I'm a nonentity to him.

When he comes back out, I say it again. "Thanks for bringing home dinner."

He sits down at the table, picks up a magazine.

"Evelyn's still in a coma."

He doesn't look at me.

"Her numbers are good, but they won't know for sure until she wakes up."

He still doesn't look at me.

"Dad, put down the magazine and talk to me."

He looks up. "What do you want me to say? What do you have to say about all this?"

"Dad, I don't know. I just—"

"What were you thinking? What have you been doing all this time? I thought I knew you—"

"Dad, you *do* know me. I'm standing right here—"

"But you did not think, Georgia. You have to think

about what others would say. What do you think they are saying, that you hang out with people like this?"

"Dad, what are you even talking about? I don't care what other people are saying. I don't have that many people, anyway."

"But your family." He's yelling now, not making any sense. "What about your family? You know what they say: It is better to lose an eye than to lose a good name."

"Dad, enough." I sit down at the table. "Can we just talk, like for real, you know?"

. . .

"Dad."

. . .

"Dad, I'm almost eighteen. I'm going to college soon. Would you talk to me? For real."

. . .

"Dad!" I yell. "I'm not a little girl anymore. Just talk to me already!"

I take a deep breath and lower my voice. "Here's the thing. I was trying things, that's all. And I'm allowed to try things. I wasn't being stupid—I mean, not that stupid. Not like what Evelyn did.

"But you—you can't put all this on me. I mean, where have you been this past year? Why do you care all of a sudden? Why weren't you caring all along?"

My dad starts to cry, really quietly, which is weird. I've only seen him cry once, on that very last day when we had to disconnect Mom from the wires, when they injected her with morphine.

He didn't cry at the wake. He didn't cry at the funeral.

And I guess I should stop talking. I guess that's enough.

But it's not.

I need to say it all.

"You should have been there for me. You should have
been asking how I was doing. You should have been listening and watching. And—" I have to say it, finally. I'm
shaking and now I'm crying, too, and I almost can't say
it, but then I do. "You should have made the decision to
take her off the machines. You should have been the one
to let her die."

He looks at me. "Oh, *koúkla mou* . . ."

"Not me. Not me, Dad."

There. I said it.

Finally.

He takes my hand.

"You're absolutely right." And when he says it, it's as
though he hadn't even realized what he'd done. "I'm so
sorry, Georgia."

"Okay, Dad." I squeeze his hand. "It's okay."

"You're just a little girl. My little girl . . ."

"No, see, here's the thing, Dad. I'm not. I'm almost
done with school and then I just have to figure out my
life. I'm going to go to college and maybe I'll drink, and
I don't know, maybe I'll get high, and I'll definitely date
guys—no, Dad, I'll date men—and I'll want to move out
at some point, and maybe I'll get married, maybe I won't,
but I have to do it all. And you have to let me, but you

also have to be there for me. You haven't really been there for me, you know?"

I say all this, and while I'm saying it, my heart is pounding pounding pounding, for it's the first time that I'm able to say exactly what I mean to my dad, and I can see from his old, sad face that it might be too much, but then he does something that lessens the deafening pounding, something that makes it all better.

This is what he does:

He places his hand on mine.

"To kseri, koúkla mou," he says. *"Katalaveno óla."*

I know, my child. I understand it all.

And I really think he does.

Tonight, it's like this:

After dinner I ask him to teach me to flambé.
He protests at first, says it's been years,
too long to remember,
but then he smiles at the thought
at the memory
at the prospect
of returning to a place
where he hasn't been
for a very long time.

We heat the oil
add the cheese
and the brandy, and

he tells me to light it.
The flames rise high
blue and gold and bright
in this small, dark kitchen
in this warm, spring night.
My father and I together,
staring into the sun.

Evelyn's mom calls at around midnight. Evelyn's okay.
She's awake and talking and groggy and in a terrible state,
but she's alive, and she's going to be okay.

She's going to be okay.

15

Sunday morning, ten A.M.

Today's the day to do it.

I pick up the phone and dial his number.

It rings and rings.

He answers.

"Hello?"

Deep breath.

"Hi, Daniel. This is Georgia."

"Oh, hi!" I can hear him smile through the phone. Isn't that a funny thing? Even in just two little words, you can tell. The tenor of the voice is so specific that that particular emotion can travel across time and distance through invisible airwaves into the human ear, into the human heart.

I do #13, again.

And he says yes.

We're going to meet (today!) for lunch and a movie and maybe something after.

I text Liss.

She texts right back with cheers and hoorays.

Time to go tell Evelyn.

Time to do something right.

I'm back at the hospital, back at the land of the almost dead, but now this girl Evelyn, who I've known for less than eight months, who texted *me* in what could have been her very last moment on this earth, is awake and alive and looking at me.

She's only barely alive, though, her arms nearly as thin as the metal rail that separates us, her eyes hollow and red and fixated on her own woven hands.

An IV drips into her veins. The machine behind her head announces the *beep beep beep* of her pulse. Tulips wilt next to her.

She's waiting for me to say something.

I don't know what to say.

At first, I stumble. I say things like "I'm glad you're okay" and "How's the food?" and "When will you get out of here?"

She gives me stilted answers like "Yeah, me too" and "Sucks big-time" and "Not for a few weeks, probably, I don't know."

I don't know what to say.

So finally, I say this:

"I'm horribly pissed at you for doing what you did."

Evelyn turns her empty eyes to look at me. It's the first time she's looking at me.

"Thanks," she says. "Real nice. Way to get mad at a sick person."

"That's not what I mean." I stumble again. I want to get this right. I need to get this right.

I reach into my bag and pull out my mom's letter. I unfold it. It's crinkled and worn from me opening and closing it so much. Besides Liss, I haven't shown it to anyone else, not even my dad.

I hand it to Evelyn. I let her read it.

She looks back at me, her eyes wide and empty, her skin tight and pale. "What does this have to do with me?"

"My mom charged me with this directive to do everything she didn't do, and I'm sort of pissed at her, too, for not doing it herself. She could have done it. She could have controlled her sugar and eaten right and walked more like she said she was going to, but she never did. Instead, she let herself gain weight and she didn't control her sugar and then she left my dad and me with the final decision to let her go. There's this 0.0001 percent chance that she could have fought the sepsis and maybe woken up and maybe lived to still be my mother, but she had signed these papers saying that if there seemed to be no chance of her living a healthy life that we should pull the plug. And it was supposed to be my dad's decision. He had power of attorney. But he froze. He was lost and sad and he didn't really understand, maybe, you know, everything that was happening, everything the doctors were saying. He looked at me and he said, 'What do you want to do?' He made me decide. I was sixteen. Fucking sixteen. I shouldn't have had to decide whether my mother lives or dies.

"But I did. I decided that I couldn't watch her like that anymore. I decided that she needed to rest. I read her letter over and over and then I told my dad to tell the doctors. I told my dad she had to die."

Evelyn looks back at the letter. I'm not sure if she's listening. I'm not sure if she can hear me.

"And, look. I can't make the decision for you. But I can tell you this . . ." I lean closer to her. "You have to live. You have people who love you. You have no other choice." I reach across the cold metal rail for her hand. Static pierces our skin, and we both pull back from the shock.

"No, you can't make the choice for me."

She hands the letter back to me.

"You're right," I say. "You're totally right. I don't have the right to be angry with you, and I can't tell you what to do, or how to live your life."

She gives me a cold, blank stare.

"All I can do is tell you that I'm here for you."

She turns her head away from me.

"Look, I was a bitch for not calling you back," I say. "I have very few people in my life. To be honest, I don't know you very well. But I like you. I want to be your friend for real. You're weird and funny and you made me do things I wouldn't have done on my own, and I never said thank you for that. So thank you."

Nothing.

"We're all allowed to fuck up, you know. We all get to make mistakes."

Still no words.

Just her and me and a crumpled letter. Wilting flowers.

She stares out the window, at the brick buildings blocking our view of the lake.

"What song is playing in your head right now?"

Evelyn looks at me and cracks a small smile.

"Beatles, of course. 'Julia.'" And then she sings a line for me. "'Half of what I say is meaningless—'"

"When you get out of here," I say, "will you finish the list with Liss and me?"

Evelyn doesn't answer immediately. Instead, she closes her eyes, and I think maybe she's fallen asleep. Her breath is steady and full, like that of a child.

After a few long, heavy minutes, she opens her eyes.

She lets me take her hand. Her skin is cold, and I can feel her bones under the thin flesh.

"Yes," she says. "I'd really, really love to."

On the way out of the hospital, I check my phone. There are three texts from Daniel:

Text #1: *How's Evelyn? Let me know.*

Text #2: *Movies are too asocial. Let's do something else.*

Text #3: *You're downtown, right? Shall we meet at the aquarium? Do you like fish?*

The first thing I notice is that he's a hypergrammatical texter, just like me.

The second thing I notice is that he wants to go to the aquarium.

He's a big dork, just like me.

Siiigh.

I text back: *Yes. That sounds perfect. Fish are fine, but I mostly love the sea horses.*

Him: *We'll find the sea horses first. We'll search for the pregnant fathers. Maybe we'll witness a live birth. Maybe we'll be asked to be godparents.*

Oh, he's ridiculously, incredibly, wonderfully awesome.

Me: *I'm naming my sea horse Vincent. He'll become a well-known master of maritime watercolors.*

I write this as a reference to one of Marquez's lectures where he showed us a bunch of Van Gogh paintings of sailboats. Crossing fingers he gets it.

Him: *Here's hoping he doesn't drink too much and cut off his own fin.*

YES.

Me: *Nice.*

Him: *Scaling back on the fish puns so soon?*

Me: *Oh my Cod. You are too much.*

Him: *See you soon.*

YES. YES. YES.

We meet out front and wait in the long line of tourists and families, and at first it's incredibly awkward, but then I ask him about college and then about his dad, and then we find our way to reciting Marquezisms and bands we like, and we both relax a bit, and I sort of have to pinch

myself that this is really happening, that I'm really on a
date with Daniel Antell. We make our way in and shuffle
through the throngs of people. We visit the sharks and
the jellies, the eels and piranhas. We find our sea horse
family and name the smallest ones after some of our favorite artists—Frida (for Kahlo), Andy (for Warhol), Keith
(for Haring), and, of course, little Vince.

We head up to a large, open amphitheater on the top
floor where the dolphins are leaping and dancing, mid-
show. Even though it's crazy crowded, we find a few
open seats in the back. Behind the dolphins' pool is a wide
wall of windows that looks east, onto Lake Michigan.

There are little kids behind us, crying because they
want to sit down, so we give them our seats and make
our way down to the lowest level, where we are in an underwater cave. We crowd in to the window to see the
dolphins and belugas. Little kids squeeze in front of us,
and the crush of adults behind us pushes us together so
that I have to angle in front of him, my back against his
chest. I want to look at the dolphins' dance, now even
more beautiful from this underwater perspective, but I'm
blinded by the touch of his body that is so close to mine.
I turn my chin to look at him, and he smiles. There's no
way I'm drooling on him this time.

"Should we get out of here?" he asks.

I nod, even though I can't imagine any other place I'd
rather be.

We make our way out of the crowded museum to the
balcony, where the wind from the lake is whipping my

hair. The show inside has ended, but we can still see the shadows of the dolphins through the amphitheater windows. It's such an odd thing, to see dolphins so close to a Midwestern lake.

"It must be so confusing for them," I say. "To swim in that pool and never get to see the ocean anymore. They must wonder where the waves are. They must wonder about the sunset. I mean, it's so sad, right? From this angle, they never get to see it—only the sunrise."

I feel like I'm rambling, filling the empty air between us with random thoughts, when he leans down and kisses me softly. It takes me by surprise at first, and I pull back. But then I take a deep breath. And I return the kiss. The wind whips wildly around us.

It's such a good first date.

We head south under the shadow of Soldier Field alongside Burnham Harbor, where we make fun of boat names (*Baby Tonga, Sail-la-Vie,* and *The Other Woman*). We come upon Sled Hill, right below the stadium. During the winter it's packed with lines of kids all waiting their turns to fly down the snow, but now it's quiet and empty, just a few sunbathers burning their skin. We climb to the top, a good thirty feet or so, take a seat. The skyline is beautiful from up here, and it's not quite as windy as down by the aquarium.

I think he's going to kiss me again.

So I kiss him first.

And it's so good.

"What do you want to do now?" he asks.

I tell him about the list (most of it). I tell him that I want to run down the hill, but I also tell him I don't know how. "I'm just freaking scared," I say.

"What are you scared of?"

I don't really want to let him know that I'm a big wimp and I'm pretty much afraid of everything, but I'm the one who started this stupid conversation, so now I have to say it. "Well, first of all, I'm scared of heights."

"Um . . ." He laughs. "This is a hill, not a mountain."

"Yeah, okay. Well, then I'm just scared of the downward perpetual motion. Of falling, plain and simple. Of tumbling down and hurting myself. Of spraining an ankle or busting a knee or something."

"Anything else?" He smiles.

"Well, no. I think that's it." I punch him lightly in the arm. "What about you? Aren't you scared of anything?"

His face changes. The smile that I love so much disappears. "Sure." He shrugs.

"Like what?"

"Losing my dad."

I nod. "Yeah. I was scared of that too, for my mom. I'm not scared of dying, though," I say. "It's worse being left behind, don't you think?"

"I don't know yet." He pauses for a moment, looking out at the lake, and then the smile returns. "But both scenarios have to be much worse than running down this hill, which will take all of six seconds."

I laugh.

"So why do you want to do it so badly, then?" he asks. "Why is this hill calling out to you?"

I have to think about this. I remember my father, when I was younger, telling me about his childhood in Greece, about how he used to run in the mountains, up and down the hills, that he was a mountain goat, a child of the woods, free and fearless. I don't ever remember feeling that way as a child. I'm a city mouse. I know nothing about running outside, let alone down a hill.

"To feel human," I say.

So Daniel shows me how to do it: The trick, as he shows me, is not to go toe-heel, toe-heel, as one might think, but to go heel-arch-ball, heel-arch-ball, just as if you were walking. He knows this from hiking with his dad in Oregon, well, before his dad got sick. "Just respect the laws of physics," he says. "Use the entire surface area of your feet, and allow gravity to be your friend."

"The laws of physics? I hardly passed chemistry. . . ."

"Just use your feet, and go slowly, at first. Then, pick up speed, and let yourself be."

I run down the hill, just like he shows me how.

It's pretty easy, when you know what to do.

And with that, I've completed numbers 1, 13, and 14 all in one day.

16

Of course, the very next day the envelope comes from the
University of Illinois.

And it's a thin one.

I sit on the front steps of my building, rip open the envelope, and skim the letter: Your application . . . blah
blah blah . . . carefully reviewed . . . blah blah blah . . .
We are sorry to inform you . . . blah blah blah . . .

Shit.

Well then.

Dad's leaving for California, so my one option is to go
with him, apply to a city college somewhere in the middle
of L.A., and see what happens from there.

My other option is . . .

I have no other options.

Just when things were turning around. Just when I
had friends again. And just when Daniel and I started

whatever it is that we're starting. Of course the letter would come today.

Daniel and Liss are going to U of I.

And I'm not.

Now what.

It's the last week of school, and we're all checked out, and the teachers could care less and everyone's talking about summer road trips and dorm rooms and prereqs for fall. I get daily texts from Liss to join her and her new friends, Avery and Chloe, and the others for lunch, and so I do. Turns out they're okay, I guess. I don't have to love them like she does, but it's nice to be included for once. What matters most is that we still have afternoons together, just her and me, and those feel like the old days.

I get hourly texts from Evelyn with little notes about the—and I quote—*shitty-ass hospital food* and the young male doctors who are *beyond sexxxy*.

And I get hourly kisses from Daniel, which are the best.

I never thought I'd be the one to say this, but I wish high school weren't ending so soon.

On the last Thursday before graduation, Marquez calls me over after class, and for once, he doesn't ask me to go sit outside on a bench. "Congratulations on a great year," he says, shaking my hand.

"Thanks."

"Sit down. What are your plans for fall?"

"Not sure." I shrug. I tell him about the U of I and my move to California. "I don't really want to go, though.

I'm not sure how I can tell my dad that. I was hoping to get accepted to U of I just so I could stay in Illinois. It would have been a great excuse. I just don't see myself as a California girl."

"What about Columbia College? They have rolling admissions. It might not be too late. Go online and fill out the application, and I'll make a couple of phone calls. I can't promise anything, but you never know. If not in the fall, maybe in the spring? You're going to do art, right?"

Oh. Wow. What?

"To be perfectly honest, I hadn't thought about what I'm going to do, but that would be amazing if you could—"

He interrupts me and puts up his hand. "You are going to do art. That much I know."

Really? Is this what I want? To be an artist?

To live the same life as her?

I watched her swim in colors and drown herself on the flat surfaces of canvas and ask questions about the universe without living in it.

I watched her sit in her studio, sketching, reading, painting, destroying—for hours and hours, days and days sometimes—disconnected from us, from her body, from what was real.

I watched her deteriorate. I watched her wither. I watched her shrivel.

Obesity, diabetes, heart disease, kidney failure, sepsis, death.

She didn't choose this life, but she didn't fight against it, either.

And here I am, an artist. Starting out, just like her.

What is it that *I* want?

"Do I have to decide right now?" I say this aloud, but I know the answer right as I finish the question.

Marquez looks surprised and, frankly, a little disappointed, but then he says finally, "No, you don't have to decide anything. You have to live your life. No one else is going to do it for you."

I hear my mom's words: *Be brave, Georgia.*

The bravest thing I could do right now is to step out into the unknown, away from her.

Maybe I will go to art school.

Maybe I won't.

But I know that there are other options. Other items that aren't on the list. Other lists, long lists, that have yet to be written.

I almost don't go to graduation because I hate last things. But I do, for my dad. I'm sweating under my polyester gown and the ceremony is cheesy and long and I can't sit for this long in the glaring sun, but in the end, when we throw our caps into the air, I can't help crying. We need finality. We need conclusions. We need to know when the old ends and the new begins.

After the ceremony and the obligatory Greektown lunch with Maria and all the cousins who drove in from the suburbs, Dad and I drive home in silence. He closed the restaurant for the day (only three weeks left until he closes it for good), so we have the whole day to ourselves, which is something we're really not used to.

"Tell me, *koúkla mou*, what now? What should we do?"

I blurt it out. "Dad, I don't want to move to California. I want to stay here in Chicago. Go to school here. Maybe live with Evelyn. Make sure she's okay. I want to live my life here." I don't even realize that this is what I want until I say it aloud. And when I say it, I know it's exactly what I need to do.

He looks over at me, and he isn't at all startled or worried or unnerved. "Okay, *koúkla*. Whatever you want. We can figure it all out in good time." He pauses. "But, I meant to say, what do you want to do today? For the rest of the afternoon?"

Oh.

I think for a moment. #8. "I want to go fishing. Do you know how?"

We stop home to change, and then he drives us up to the North Side, where we rent fishing gear and stroll along the Des Plaines River, where the forest preserves drown out the suburbs.

He shows me how to hold the rod and cast the line and how to sit quietly and wait. We catch a few pike—they are golden, stolid creatures—and then we unhook their mouths and throw them back in.

"Dad," I say as we're packing up the car, "I'd like to go skydiving, too."

He plants a kiss on my forehead. "Not today, *koúkla*. Maybe tomorrow."

Somehow, I've made it this far. And now, somehow, despite all my deeply ingrained fears, I have to learn how to swing from four ropes twenty-five feet off the ground.

Shit.

But I made a promise to myself.

And to my friends.

With the money I earned from my painting sales, I offered to pay for their trapeze lessons if they would do it with me. There's a place on the lakefront where they teach you how to fly. "Come be a monkey with me," I told them. Of course, they were all in, no questions asked.

So two weeks after graduation, a mere three weeks after my grand art debut and my reunion with Liss and Evelyn's shaky return to our world and my first kiss with Daniel, I'm here, suspended upside down, with all of Chicago inverted around me.

And this is what it's like:

I'm oscillating from one end of the ladder to the other.

The net is so very far below my head.

The blood rushes to my head and

my friends, they call out to me, and

I'm screaming and

laughing and

howling

above the world.

The entire city moves under me.
It's all there, waiting.
I'm marking air,
I'm moving time.
The molecules around me sway and
bump and
move right along
with me.

I'm doing everything.
I'm doing it all, Mom.
Even more than you could have ever imagined.

For me, and
for you.

ACKNOWLEDGMENTS

Thank you to Rose Hilliard, for your guidance, encouragement, and excitement. Thanks to everyone at St. Martin's Press, including Jen Enderlin, Anne Marie Tallberg, Michelle Cashman, Emily Walters, and Lizzie Poteet. Olga Grlic, thank you for the beautiful cover. A thank-you to Courtney Miller-Callihan, for your wisdom and grace; also, special thanks to everyone at Sanford J. Greenburger Associates.

So much gratitude to my soul sisters, Kate Eberle (also *the* very first reader), Aimee Kandelman, and Kara Noe. To my first readers, Pamela Zimny and J. A. Ward, who encouraged me to take the leap to send this story out into the world. Thank you to my California family: "Papa" Ray Elias, Chuck Bush, Karnit Galmidi (bubba), Michael Braun, Mandy Berkowitz, Jon Berkowitz, Hannah Maximova, Michael Hartigan, and Tessa Taylor. This also includes my Yoga Blend family: Christy Marsden, Bekah

Turner, Nicole Honnig, and absolutely everyone at the studio. Thanks to my family in Chicago and Greece. Special long-distance hugs to Shirley Mann, for the weekly calls, candles, and "attagirls." I am grateful to be surrounded by so much love.

I am eternally grateful to the Society of Children's Book Writers and Illustrators. Special thanks to Francesca Rusackas and Q. L. Pearce at the SCBWI SoCal chapter. Also, thanks to my writer friends, Lori Polydoros, Kathleen Green, Teri Keeler, Hilde Garcia, Amy Elaine Mills-Klipstine, Amaris Glass, Autumn Hilden, Farrah Penn, Frey Hoffman, and Antonio Borrego. Robyn Schneider, thank you for your good advice. Corrie Shatto, thank you for your friendship. Your spirit is a gift in my life. Over the past year, the YA Binders have added another amazing dimension to my community. To my writing teachers, Noel Alumit, Mandy Hubbard, and Margo Dill, thank you for your honest feedback and guidance. Thanks to the UCLA Extension and LitReactor for the fantastic classes. Thanks to my friends and colleagues at Pasadena City College and to my students for your constant curiosity and openness.

This book is also dedicated to my parents, Ted and Eleanor Kottaras. I miss you.

Finally, to the two loves of my life, Matthew and Madeline. In the moments that I am brave, it's because of you.

If you or someone you love is thinking about suicide, please call

1-800-273-TALK (8255)

The National Suicide Prevention Lifeline is available to help.

For more information about warning signs and resources, visit

www.suicidepreventionlifeline.org